THE
CONTENDERS

THE
CONTENDERS

By
Peg Cheng

Reading rocks!

Peg Cheng

This novel is a work of fiction. Any references to real locales, establishments, organizations, or events are intended only to give the story a sense of authenticity. All other names, places, characters, and incidents portrayed in this book are the product of the author's imagination.

The author greatly appreciates you taking the time to read her work. Please consider leaving a review wherever you found the book, or telling your friends about *The Contenders*, to help spread the word. Thank you for supporting independent authors.

ISBN: 978-1-943578-00-9

Cover design by Kit Foster

For Nic, Nate, Noah, and Logan

CONTENTS

1. YANG VS. WARFIELD

Eunice Yang scowled as she stood under the old oak tree in the backyard. The September sun blazed, making her black hair feel like it was on fire. She jumped up and grabbed the lowest branch. It was too dang hot to be doing pull-ups, but she had to do them every day. And every time she did, she wished her classmate Thad Warfield dead.

Thad was short for a ten-year-old, wiry and fast like a coyote. With unruly, blond curls and a freckled face, he looked like the poster boy for the Washington apple industry. At first glance, you thought you could whip him. Last year, Henry Evans, a sixth grader, made that assumption. Henry was a head taller and twenty pounds heavier. It was like watching a half-starved wild animal take down a fat, slobbering Labrador. Poor Henry never knew what hit him.

"Ten," Eunice puffed as she pulled her chin over the branch one last time before dropping to the grass. She tapped a button on her watch. Fourteen seconds. Not bad.

Eunice brushed her hands together. They were calloused and rough as a tree trunk. Most ten-year-olds would hate to have hands like these, especially the girls, but Eunice was secretly proud of them. She remembered when she had first tried doing a pull-up when she was six. She hung there for what seemed like hours, willing herself to move. She couldn't. Not one inch.

She lay down on the grass, crossed her arms across her chest, and bent her knees. After fifty sit-ups, she flopped back on the grass to catch her breath. When she had rested a few minutes, she put on her pink-and-black high-top sneakers, got up, grabbed her bike, and wheeled it around the house to the street.

Eunice smiled as she rode toward the shores of Soap Lake. It wasn't because she could see all the tourists covered with mud, looking like pigs after a good wallow. It wasn't because she was riding her rickety old bike. And it wasn't because she loved the feel of the sun warming her skin as she breathed in the disturbing yet comforting rotten-egg smell of the lake's mineral-rich waters. Eunice smiled because this was the year she could enter The Contest. This was the year she'd get back at Thad Warfield for good.

Officially it was the Soap Lake Brawn and Brains Contest, but everyone just called it The Contest. Only fifth graders could compete because, a long time ago, kids stopped going to school after fourth grade to work on the family farm. The Contest was a way to get kids to stay in school for another year. Practically all of the 1,826 people living in Soap Lake showed up to watch the competitions—everyone, that is, except Eunice's neighbor, Mrs. Lebowitz. Mrs. Lebowitz never stepped foot out of her yard.

Eunice stopped at the edge of the sandy shore and watched little kids and old people slather themselves with the black, goopy mud from the bottom of the lake. During the summer, people came from miles around to soak in the water and glop themselves with mud. They believed it was a magical cure for their health problems. Eunice remembered the story she had heard in first grade about an old woman from Russia whose arthritis was so bad she couldn't walk. After a summer of soaking in the lake, she was able to stroll up and down the beach.

Too bad mud glopping wasn't one of The Contest's competitions. She remembered the mud fight that broke out after school on the last day of first grade. Eunice and her best friend, Jenny, were superior mud flingers, better than most of the boys. Eunice grinned, then shook off the memory. Thinking back on first grade always made Eunice's stomach hurt. The Incident happened in first grade. The Incident was what convinced Eunice that she needed to win The Contest.

Eunice pushed off and rode down Main Avenue, stopping outside Bob's Bicycle Shop, which had floor-to-ceiling windows all around. Eunice did not go to church, but she worshipped at Bob's every Sunday, sometimes Tuesdays too. It was the most beautiful shop in all of Soap Lake, maybe in all of Washington. Eunice got off her bike and swung the kickstand down. She stood close to the window, her breath creating a circle of fog.

When The Contest first started, the winner received a cow or a pig. Farm animals were a big deal back then. Now the winner got his or her name engraved on a plaque in city hall; their picture in the *Soap Lake Bugle*; and best of all, any bicycle from Bob's Bicycle Shop. Even though most Soap Lake parents couldn't afford to buy a bike from Bob's— they sold mostly to tourists—every kid had a favorite picked out.

Eunice knew exactly which bike she'd choose.

The cherry Rainier Cruiser.

Shiny red metallic paint that glinted with golden specks in the sunlight. A silver bike bell with a red cherry painted on it attached to the left side of the handlebar. A little black wire basket in front to hold books, lunch, and other important things. And white wall tires so fat and full of air, you could pedal your way to the moon.

Eunice was saving her allowance to buy the cherry bike bell. Even if she had to wait the whole school year to win the Cruiser, she could put the bell on her old bike. If she was good and didn't spend her allowance, she could have it by New Year's.

Eunice closed her eyes and imagined herself taking off on that beautiful Cruiser. She'd wave to the townspeople, her hair blowing in the breeze and the sun on her skin. As she rode by, they'd whisper, "Awesome bike. Totally awesome."

CRASH!

Eunice's eyes flew open. She turned around to see her bike—with chipped black paint and rusty fenders—sprawled on the sidewalk, its skinny wheels spinning. Her face flamed.

Thad Warfield and his best friend, Buzz, stood in front of her, smirks on their faces. "Hey, Eun-i-cycle," Thad said. "Still riding that ugly bike?"

Eunice crouched down and picked her bike up off the sidewalk. She stuck out her chin. "At least it's not as ugly as you."

Buzz laughed. Thad slapped his arm. Buzz stopped laughing.

"Can't Daddy afford to buy you a new one? Oh, wait, that's right. He's a waiter."

Eunice lunged at Thad. "Shut up about my dad!" She swung wildly, but Buzz yanked her back, holding her arms. She struggled to get loose.

Thad clicked his tongue and shook his head. "Good thing I don't hit girls or you'd have a black eye right now."

"I'll give you a black eye!" Eunice wrenched her arms out, but Buzz grabbed them again and pinned them behind her.

"I bet you would." Thad's voice was so calm and steady, it made Eunice madder. "Yep, I bet you would."

Eunice struggled and cursed herself silently for not being strong enough to break free. She vowed to work up to fifteen pull-ups by the end of the month.

Thad watched her struggle for a minute, then waved his hand. "Let her go."

Buzz released her, and she lurched forward. Her upper arms hurt, but she refused to rub them in front of these jerks. She glared at Buzz, then fixed a deadly eye on Thad. "I'm going to beat you."

"Beat me in what?"

"The Contest."

Thad and Buzz burst out laughing. Thad held his stomach like it hurt. "That's a good one, Eun-i-cycle!" They continued to snicker as they shuffled down the street.

Eunice watched them go, trying to think of a good one-liner to lob at their sniggering backs. But her arms hurt. Her chest pounded. And her eyes stung.

She got on her bike and pedaled away hard. She'd never felt surer about anything in her whole life. She'd win The Contest, no matter what. She just had to win.

2. A YANG FAMILY TRADITION

Eunice rode down Buttercup Street and pulled up in front of a little blue house. It was the smallest house on the street. The paint was fading, but the brown lawn was trimmed neat as a carpet. She wheeled through the chain link gate to the backyard and propped her bike under the eaves. The bike's paint was chipped even more after the fall. Tears formed in her eyes, but she blinked them back.

Walking around to the back, Eunice saw her father through the kitchen window. He waved at her, his hand white with flour. She came through the back door, the screen slamming behind her. Her dad was mixing dough in a bowl on the kitchen counter. Eunice pulled up a stool and sat down, slumping her shoulders.

Her father stopped mixing and looked at her. "What's up, kid?"

Eunice sighed. "Thad Warfield is the most evil boy on earth, and I hate his guts, and I'm going to beat him to a *pulp* in The Contest."

"When have I heard that before?" He went back to mixing.

"I wish he was dead."

Dad cleared his throat. "Eunice—"

"Dead. DEAD. *DEAD*."

"It's not good to put a death wish on anyone."

"You don't understand. He hates me. He's out to get me."

"You out to get him?"

"Dad!"

He held up both hands. "Okay, okay. Thad Warfield is the most evil boy on earth."

Eunice sighed, leaned on the counter, and cupped her chin in her hand. Her dad understood a lot of things, but this one he didn't. Watching him mix the dough, Eunice's thoughts floated back to that day in first grade.

She had been playing hopscotch with Jenny after lunch. Some boys were on the basketball court, bragging about who would win The Contest for their year. Thad, of course, was the loudest. Just as Eunice bent down on one foot to pick up her hopscotch marker, Thad barreled by to retrieve a ball and knocked her off-balance. She sprawled on the ground. The boys laughed.

"Watch it, Eun-i-cycle," Thad sneered.

"You watch it! And don't call me Eun-i-cycle!"

"Okay, Eun-i-cycle," Thad said, making a face. The boys laughed.

Eunice got up and dusted herself off. Her face burned. She hated people laughing at her. Before she knew it, she blurted out, "I'm going to win The Contest, you know."

Thad laughed. "You can't win."

"Why not?"

"Because no one like you has ever won."

Jenny stepped up next to her. "Liar. Girls have won before." Eunice swelled with pride at her friend's loyalty.

"I don't mean girls," Thad said, pointing at Eunice's face. "I mean people who look like her." He pulled back on the corners of his eyes until they were slits and sang out, "Ching chong! Ching chong!"

The boys laughed and imitated Thad. Eunice didn't know what to say. Her face felt like it would go up in flames. The recess bell rang and they all scrambled to get in line.

It hadn't bothered her before when she thought about herself and Dad being the only Asian people in all of Soap Lake. But now it felt different. Ever since that day, some of the boys pulled their eyes back when they saw her and said that awful chant. It made her want to cry and punch them at the same time. When she told her dad about it, he told her to ignore them and they would stop. After a long while it finally did stop, but she never forgot about it. And she never forgot who started it.

"Earth to Eunice," Dad said, waving at her. Eunice blinked and came to. Her stomach felt crushed, like a stuck accordion. She breathed out and tried to relax. It hurt to let go. "Thad's jealous of you."

Eunice scowled and shook her head.

"What? You're smart. You're pretty. You're the fastest runner in school. And your dad's the best baker in town."

"Carson's the fastest."

"Correction. You're smart, pretty, the second-fastest runner in school, and your dad's the best baker in town."

Eunice shook her head. He didn't understand. He had grown up in Taiwan where everyone had the same eyes.

Dad pinched off pieces of dough and rolled them between his palms into little balls. "Are you going to sit there, or are you going to help out your old man?"

"You're not old," Eunice muttered as she slipped off the stool and went to wash her hands.

"You remember how to do it?"

"You've shown me a million times." Eunice dried her hands on a towel and got a dish from the cupboard. She filled it with white sugar. She took a bottle of cinnamon from the spice shelf and added three spoonfuls to the sugar. She found a bottle of fragrant, dark brown spice and added a half spoonful. She mixed it all together until the sugar turned light brown.

Eunice joined her father at the counter. After he rolled the dough into little balls, she dropped them into the spiced sugar and coated them all around. Working together in silence, they filled three cookie sheets with sugared dough balls.

While her dad washed the dishes and utensils, Eunice sat back on the stool and watched. It was comforting to watch him cook, bake, and clean. Part of what he had said was true. He was the best baker and cook in the whole town, probably the whole county. Too bad his boss at the Lucky Dragon didn't believe it. Dad should have been the chef instead of the waiter. But life isn't always fair, as he often reminded her.

Eunice's stomach growled. "What's for dinner?"

Dad avoided her gaze and started laying waxed paper into two shoeboxes.

"Can we make chow mein?" It was a Yang family tradition to cook a special meal together the night before school started and then watch *60 Minutes* on TV.

Even though her dad usually worked on Sundays, he always took this one Sunday off.

Dad stopped fussing with the boxes and put his hands on Eunice's shoulders. "I'm sorry, but Hal's sick. I have to go in. I'll make it up to you tomorrow night." He gave her shoulders a squeeze. "I need your help delivering the snickerdoodles."

"Can't I do it tomorrow?"

"You know Mr. Oliver and Mrs. Lebowitz expect them tonight." Eunice crossed her arms. "You're ten. You're old enough to do the deliveries on your own now."

Eunice kicked the rung on the stool with her heel. Another Yang family tradition down the drain. The day before school started, Eunice and her dad always delivered cookies to Mr. Oliver and Mrs. Lebowitz. It was the neighborly thing to do, her dad said.

Eunice didn't mind delivering cookies on her own to Mr. Oliver. He was a nice old man who always smelled of Old Spice cologne. She liked his bloodhound, Watson, too. But she didn't like Mrs. Lebowitz. She was scary. The kids had nicknamed her the Black Widow because her husband was dead and she always wore black. She never left her house except to look for spiders in the yard. She never even shopped for groceries. What did she eat? Spiders?

Mrs. Lebowitz didn't like her either. She never smiled whenever Eunice saw her. Not even a little half smile. Nothing. Eunice was convinced she was a witch.

"I know what you're thinking," Dad said.

"You do not."

"She's not a witch." Eunice looked away from him, trying not to smile. "And don't call her the Black Widow either." Dad gave Eunice a warning look. "She's just a lonely old lady. You respect your elders."

Eunice nodded, even though she didn't completely agree with him. She didn't think she had to respect elders who didn't respect her.

"Remember to set the timer. And let the cookies cool before you put them in the boxes." Dad checked the oven. "Dinner's in the fridge." Eunice was still sulky. He chucked her chin. "Okay?" Eunice reached up, grabbed his shoulders in a hug, and jumped off the stool at the same time. "Oof," Dad said, stumbling back. "You're getting too old for stuff like this." He lowered her to the ground and gave her a kiss on the forehead. "If you need anything—"

"I know, I know," Eunice said. "Call Mr. Oliver."

"Lights out at nine. I'll call Mr. Oliver to make sure you do it."

The front door closed. She walked to the stove, crouched down, and flipped on the oven light. The balls of dough had spread into perfect little circles on the sheets. She breathed in. Even with the comforting, delicious smell of warm spices filling her nose, Eunice couldn't stop her stomach from doing flip-flops.

She's not a witch, she reminded herself. She's *not* a witch.

3. SPECIAL DELIVERY

When Eunice stepped out of the house into the cool evening air, the sky was like a canvas streaked with pink and purple. She took a picture of it with her mind. Click. Recorded forever. Satisfied, she carried two shoeboxes filled with snickerdoodles to the brick house next door and rang the doorbell.

A man in his late sixties opened the door. He was thin with neat gray hair and a goatee, wearing pressed jeans and a sweatshirt printed with *The Secret's In the Mud*. A large bloodhound ambled to his side, his tongue lolling out. The man's eyes crinkled into half-moons.

"What ho, Eunice!" Mr. Oliver said, breaking into a huge grin. Eunice loved his accent. He was from England, or "across the Pond," as he liked to say.

"Special delivery from the Yang Bakery."

Eunice handed him one of the shoeboxes. He cracked open the top, closed his eyes, and inhaled deeply. "Five-spice snickerdoodles. It's not September without them." He opened his eyes and peeked behind her. "Where's your dad?"

"He had to go in. Hal's sick."

Mr. Oliver shook his head. "Hardest working man in Soap Lake."

"Yeah," Eunice said, secretly wishing her dad wasn't so hardworking.

Watson snuffled at the box. Mr. Oliver waved at him to go back inside. "If you're good, Watson, you might get one." He winked at Eunice. "That is, if I don't eat them all myself. Goodness, where are my manners? Won't you come in for some steak and kidney pie?"

Eunice stopped herself from making a face at the mention of kidneys. "No, thank you."

"Some tea then?"

"Thanks, but I've got another delivery to do, and then I have to get ready for school."

He shook his head. "I can't believe it's here already."

Eunice looked wistful. "Summer went so fast."

"Summer? I meant the last decade. Just yesterday you were in diapers, and your dad was moving in next door after your mother passed. Now you're old enough to be in The Contest."

Why did grown-ups always think time went so fast? Mr. Oliver's eyes were moist. Eunice smiled. "Will you come watch me?"

Mr. Oliver dabbed at his eyes with a handkerchief. "Wouldn't miss it for the world." A woof came from inside the house. "Watson too." He patted the shoebox. "Thank you for the cookies, dear girl. Give my regards to your father."

Eunice waved. "See ya, Mr. Oliver."

The sky darkened as Eunice walked past her house and over to the house on the other side. Unlike Mr. Oliver's cheerful brick house, Mrs. Lebowitz's house was the kind that made you want to walk faster as you passed it. Eunice couldn't tell what color it used to be because the siding had turned dark gray with years of dirt and dust. The hedges were so overgrown that she had to walk one foot in front of the other, like on a tightrope, to stay on the sidewalk.

Eunice hesitated at the rusty gate, debating whether to turn and run. Just as she thought of an excuse to give her dad, Thad's face appeared, taunting her. "If you weren't a girl, you'd have a black eye right now." At times like this, Thad had an annoying way of popping into her mind. Would *he* run away?

Eunice sighed and pushed open the gate. A few more steps and she was on the creaky front porch. She took a deep breath. As she reached toward the doorbell, the door flew open. Her heart jumped into her throat.

Standing right in front of her was the Black Widow, looking even older than Eunice remembered. Her face was all wrinkled, like an old apple. Her gray hair was pulled tightly back in a bun. She wore a black T-shirt and a long black jumper that reached almost to the ground. To her amazement, Eunice spied pink-and-black-striped stocking feet peeking out beneath the hem. One striped foot tapped the floor.

"Don't you know it's rude to stare?"

Eunice held out the box of cookies. The old woman snatched them from her hands.

"Joe's five-spice snickerdoodles," Mrs. Lebowitz whispered, holding the box up to her nose. She closed her eyes for a second, breathing in the spicy goodness. Her eyes flashed open. "You don't like me, do you?"

"I don't know you," Eunice said.

"Exactly." She turned on her striped heel and slammed the door.

Eunice froze in shock. When she came to, she sped back to her house, locked the door, ran to her bedroom, and flung herself onto her bed, her heart beating like mad.

Sitting back against her pillows, Eunice surveyed the room. The pale yellow walls. Her purple desk that had been off-white and full of stains when her dad first bought it at a garage sale. A black flag printed with a skull and crossbones hanging above the desk. Her bedside table, also painted by her dad, but this time in black-and-white stripes. On top of it sat an alarm clock, a lamp, and a thick book called *The History of Pirates*. A yellowed map on top of the book. Her heart began to beat normally again.

Why'd she have to slam the door in my face? Totally rude!

Eunice shook her head, jumped up from the bed, and stomped toward the kitchen, out the screen door, and into the backyard. She turned to face the fence that bordered her house and the Black Widow's.

"I'm not afraid of you, Mrs. Lebowitz!" Eunice yelled. "And by the way, you're welcome for the cookies!"

Respect your elders. How about respecting me?

As she turned to go back in the house, Eunice heard something. She paused. There it was again: a soft chuckle from the other side of the fence followed by the sound of munching.

JOE'S FIVE-SPICE SNICKERDOODLES
Makes three dozen

2 cups all-purpose flour
2 teaspoons cream of tartar
1 teaspoon baking soda
¼ teaspoon salt
2 sticks unsalted butter, softened (save the waxed
    paper wrappers)
1½ cups white sugar
2 large eggs
½ cup white sugar
4 teaspoons ground cinnamon
½ teaspoon five-spice powder

1. Preheat the oven to 350 degrees.
2. Grease two cookie sheets with the waxed paper
    wrappers that the butter came in.
3. Mix together the flour, cream of tartar, baking
    soda, and salt.
4. Beat the butter and 1½ cups of sugar together
    until they are very fluffy.
5. Add the eggs and beat until well combined.
6. Add the flour mixture to the butter mixture and
    mix well until smooth.

7. In a small dish or bowl, mix the ½ cup sugar with the cinnamon and five-spice powder until well blended.

8. Pull off pieces of dough and roll between the palms of your hands to form balls about the size of a large walnut. Roll the dough balls in the spiced sugar and place about 2½ inches apart on the cookie sheets.

9. Bake one sheet at a time until the cookies are light brown at the edges, about 8-11 minutes.

10. Remove the cookie sheet to a cooling rack or onto some potholders.

11. Let the cookies rest for a minute or two, then transfer them using a spatula to cooling racks or plates to cool.

12. Let the sheet cool for a few minutes before you put on the next set of cookie dough balls, or else the heated sheet will cause your dough to spread out too much in the oven.

NOTE: If you're allergic to eggs, use two tablespoons of ground flaxseed mixed with six tablespoons of warm water instead. You can buy flaxseeds at some grocery stores or in the bulk section of most health food stores. Also, if you're allergic to dairy products (milk, cream, etc.), substitute nondairy margarine for the butter.

4. MORE IMPORTANT THAN PIRATES

With the shrill ring of the school bell, kids scrambled across the blacktop like cockroaches when the basement lights are turned on. Eunice sped across the playground in her pink-and-black high-tops, her hair flying and her backpack bouncing. She got in line behind a girl with hair the color of corn silk.

"Hey, Jenny."

"Hey," Jenny said, glancing back at Eunice.

"Check this out." Eunice rifled in her backpack and brought out the yellowed map from her bedroom. She unrolled it. "It's a pirate map. My dad found it at a garage sale."

Jenny turned to whisper to the girl in front of her. Eunice scowled, scrunching her forehead, and tapped Jenny's shoulder. "I thought you liked pirates."

Jenny sniffed. "Pirates are so fourth grade."

"Since when?" Eunice said, rolling the map back up.

"Since Anna and I went to summer camp and learned about things that are"—she and Anna exchanged glances—"more important."

Jenny and Anna giggled and turned their backs. Eunice's face burned. She knew about summer camp. It wasn't real summer camp where the kids slept in the woods and roasted marshmallows at night. It was summer afternoon camp at the church on Main Avenue. Eunice had wanted to go with Jenny, but when she had asked her dad, he said no. He said that she needed to be older. Eunice was confused, since lots of kids she knew started going to church when they were babies. Her dad said she needed to know if it was right for her before she went. How could she know it was right if she never went?

Eunice thought things might go back to normal when school started, but the more Jenny and Anna whispered with each other, the more her hope slipped away. Last year, Eunice's class had read the popular series about a boy who goes to wizarding school. Anna and another classmate, Sergey, hadn't been allowed to read it. Turned out their parents didn't want their kids reading about "witchcraft." At the time, Eunice and Jenny had felt sorry for Anna.

Eunice didn't feel sorry for Anna anymore. Not one bit.

Jenny didn't have her hair pulled up in her usual ponytail but instead wore it down. Anna's hair hung long down her back too. Eunice reached up to tuck her own chin-length hair behind her ears. What was more important than pirates? She was about to ask Jenny when a tall woman with green-rimmed glasses came to the doorway.

"Good morning, ladies and gentlemen. Welcome to the fifth grade. I am Ms. Hobart. Follow me."

Eunice followed the line of kids snaking their way into the classroom. The desks and chairs were arranged in neat rows, and each desk had a paper name tent propped on top. Eunice groaned when she saw her desk assignment. Eunice, being a Yang, was always in the last desk in the last row. Thad, a Warfield, was always seated in front of her or next to her. Every year, Eunice wished the room was in reverse alphabetical order so that the Ys sat at the front of the room instead of in the back. Then the teacher could see how evil Thad was. She wished for the same seating arrangement every year, but it never happened.

Eunice slid into the desk labeled *Eunice Yang*. She dumped her backpack on the carpet. As soon as she sat down, Thad slinked by and knocked her name tent off her desk.

"Hey!" Eunice bent down to retrieve the tent, then stood up to face Thad. "Watch it, Warfield."

"Make me."

If Eunice's cheeks got any redder, they would burst into flames. She and Thad stood eye-to-eye, glaring at each other. Eunice made a fist with her right hand. She felt a warm hand on her shoulder and looked up to see Ms. Hobart. "Please take your seat, Ms. Yang. You too, Mr. Warfield." There was a warning in Ms. Hobart's voice.

Eunice sat down. She'd get Thad at recess. She made a face at him and felt better. She unzipped her backpack and took out a sheet of paper. She wrote, "What's more important than pirates?" She folded up the note, then leaned forward and tossed it on Jenny's desk.

Jenny opened the note, read it, wrote something back, and folded it back up. She yawned, stretching her arms up and back, and dropped the note onto Eunice's desk.

Eunice snatched the note and opened it. There was just one word.

BOYS.

5. THE KEY TO SUCCESS

That one word burned in Eunice's head as she filed into the gym with the rest of Soap Lake Elementary, kindergarten through fifth grade, for the first-day-of-school assembly. Eunice sat down next to Jenny and Anna.

Boys. Really? Seriously?

She longed to talk to Jenny like they used to. She'd get to the bottom of why she'd changed her mind about pirates.

Eunice eyed Anna, giggling and tossing back her long, wavy hair. Acid bubbled in her stomach. She comforted herself by remembering that Anna came from a family of freaks that wouldn't even let her read the most popular book in school.

Something hit the back of Eunice's head. She reached around and pulled a slimy spitball out of her hair. "Gross!" she said, flicking it on the floor. She spun around to see who the culprit was. No one seemed to be paying attention, but Thad and Buzz were trying way too hard not to laugh. Eunice wished Thad Warfield dead for the millionth time.

Jenny leaned over. "Thad likes to bother you."

"Lucky me," Eunice said, shaking her head.

"Maybe he likes you."

Eunice's mouth dropped open. She didn't know what to say. Her friend had lost her marbles. Jenny giggled and turned back to Anna. Eunice decided right then and there that she was glad they weren't best friends anymore. She didn't want a boy-crazy dumbhead for a best friend.

Mr. Moss, the principal, stood at the microphone. He tapped it with his finger, grinning. "Is this thing on?"

The students groaned. Mr. Moss did this at every assembly. It cracked him up. Even though it was cheesy, Eunice smiled. She liked Mr. Moss. The skin around his eyes crinkled when he smiled. Crow's feet, they were called. Eunice couldn't wait to have some herself.

"Welcome, everyone, to another year at Soap Lake Elementary!"

Everyone cheered. Mr. Moss introduced each of the teachers, the librarian, the janitor, the lunch ladies, the tech guy, and the school secretary. Each of them stood at the front of the stage and waved. Ms. Hobart was taller than all of the other women. In fact, she was as tall as Jerry, the tech guy, who was at least six feet tall.

Eunice was wondering what it would feel like to be a giant when she felt another spitball hit her, this time against the back of her neck. She felt sick at the thought of Thad's spit touching her skin. She didn't turn around this time. She wasn't going to give him the satisfaction. Instead, she would throw a jelly ball at his head at recess. She'd wipe that stupid smirk right off his face.

After some more announcements, Mr. Moss cleared his throat. "Your attention, please, ladies and gentlemen. May I present Sherry Mathers of Bob's Bicycle Shop!"

Sherry came into the gym, wheeling a shiny red bicycle with white wall tires. The cheers and applause were deafening. Eunice's heart leapt. It was her bike! The cherry Rainier Cruiser! It was the boy's model, but that was okay. Eunice took this as a sign. It was definitely a sign.

After Sherry took a turn around the stage, she stopped next to Mr. Moss and leaned into the mic. "Bob's Bicycles is delighted to sponsor the fifth grade Brawn and Brains Contest once again. May the best contender win!"

Mr. Moss smiled at her. "Thank you, Sherry. And now, please give a round of applause for Mayor Wilkinson."

A lanky man in his fifties, wearing a button-down shirt with a bolo tie, faded jeans, and cowboy boots, stepped up to the mic. "The winner of the Brawn and Brains Contest will have his or her name engraved on a plaque in city hall. And this year, the winner will also get lunch with me at any restaurant in Soap Lake."

There were only four restaurants in Soap Lake. None of them could compare to Dad's cooking. Eunice hoped the mayor considered the Scoop Shop a restaurant. She'd order the hot fudge sundae with chopped peanuts and extra cherries.

Mayor Wilkinson left the mic, and Mr. Moss launched into describing The Contest. "The first event will be the obstacle course in October. The committee has worked hard to make sure the course is different every year. It will take place as usual at the Lava Links Pitch-and-Putt."

All the kids cheered. They loved watching the obstacle course.

"The second event will be a five-minute speech given in the gym in January."

Eunice and the rest of the fifth graders groaned. No one liked giving speeches. Teachers and grown-ups loved them though. Go figure. They were the ones on the committee.

"The last event will be the science fair in May. It will take place as usual in the gym. Contenders will explain their science projects to anyone who comes by." Mr. Moss cleared his throat. "In the case of a tie, which only happened once in 1971, there will be a sudden-death elimination challenge."

Oohs and aahs rippled through the crowd. Everyone loved the idea. "Sudden death" sounded scary and wonderful at the same time. What kind of challenge would it be? Battling sharks in a tank? Walking across hot coals?

"All events are open to the public, so let's do our best to represent Soap Lake Elementary." Mr. Moss cupped his hand around his ear. "Who are we?"

Everyone in the audience flapped their arms. "The Soap Lake Eagles!"

Mr. Moss smiled. "That's right, Eagles!" He held up his hand. "Just one more bit of news. This year, on the occasion of the one hundredth anniversary of The Contest, the school board has created a new rule." He paused for effect. "This year, there will be *two* winners of The Contest!"

Everyone whooped and stomped their feet. Two winners? They'd never done that before. It was always a fight to the finish. Would that mean two people would win bicycles? Eunice's eyes shined.

Mr. Moss held up his hand again. "The school board has decided that this year's motto will be *Teamwork is the Key to Success*. This year, fifth graders will compete in teams of two."

Eunice's heart dropped into her stomach. Work in teams? It was the stupidest thing she'd ever heard.

On the way out of the gym and back to the classroom, all the fifth graders chattered about who would get matched with whom. Jenny and Anna giggled and compared what they were going to wear for the obstacle course. Buzz and Thad high-fived each other.

Was everyone nuts? Teamwork wasn't the key to success. *Winning* was the key to success. This new rule sucked. Was she the only one who knew that?

Back in the classroom, Ms. Hobart stood at the front and held up an old straw hat. It was misshapen and beat-up, like the hat Mrs. Lebowitz wore when she pored over her spider-infested bushes.

"This was my grandfather's hat. He won The Contest seventy years ago."

Ms. Hobart, the giant, was related to someone who had won The Contest?

"I thought it'd be nice to draw your names out of his hat." She swept a stack of paper slips from the edge of her desk into the hat. She held it out to Callie Hernandez, who sat in the first row. "Please mix up the names, Callie." Eunice scowled to herself. Teacher's pet already. Callie reached in and mixed up the slips.

Eunice squirmed in her seat. Maybe she'd get paired with one of the Hernandez twins. They were a pair of Goody-Two-Shoes, but they were also smart and fast, and that's what she cared about.

Ms. Hobart pulled out two slips. "Jenny Sanders"—she paused—"and Anna Kozlov." Jenny and Anna squealed with delight. They ran over and hugged each other. "Ladies," Ms. Hobart said, "please return to your seats."

If Eunice were a better person, she'd feel happy for them. But she didn't. Eunice couldn't wait to get paired up with anyone, just so she could beat those two. It didn't matter that Jenny used to be her best friend. They were contenders now.

"Jules West and Marty Patterson."

Jules and Marty whooped. Eunice bit her lip. The class nerds. They'll be impossible to beat in the science fair. But she relaxed a little when she remembered that neither one of them could run or jump worth a dang.

With every pair of names, Eunice's stomach flipped over like a dog doing tricks for a biscuit. She could hardly sit still. She crossed her legs and her fingers under her desk and hoped she would be picked next.

Ms. Hobart plucked two more slips from the hat. "Callie Hernandez and—I can't believe this—Carson Hernandez!"

Callie and Carson high-fived. Eunice groaned with the rest of the class. The Contest was as good as over. Callie and Carson were almost as good at schoolwork as the nerds, and they were definitely much better runners. On top of that, they were twins and could practically read each other's minds.

Eunice scanned the room. The only students left were Drusila, Jesus, and—

"Eunice Yang"—Eunice's heart jumped into her throat—"and Thad Warfield."

The room became eerily silent. Eunice thought she'd gone deaf. Her body froze. Everyone turned to look at her and Thad as if in slow motion.

After what seemed like an eternity, Eunice snapped back to reality. She turned to face Thad. For once, he wasn't making a face at her. She could tell from the look on his face that they felt—probably for the first time in their lives—exactly the same way.

They were doomed. Totally doomed.

6. JUST TERRIBLE

Eunice's high-tops felt like they were filled with cement. Somehow, she dragged herself home. Luckily, it
was only a ten-minute walk from school.

A dog woofed at her as she shuffled down the
street. Watson was standing with his front paws on
Mr. Oliver's perfectly trimmed boxwoods. He
strained to lick Eunice, drool running down the side
of his mouth and his tongue hanging out. Eunice kept
her distance. She liked Watson but wasn't a fan of his
drool.

Mr. Oliver looked up from trimming his bushes.
He wore a T-shirt that said *Masquers Theater: Unleash
the Drama!* "What ho, what ho! How was the first
day?"

Eunice didn't have the energy to lie. "Terrible.
Just terrible."

"Love your droll sense of humor, dear girl," he
chuckled, and went back to trimming. Watson gave a
farewell woof and flopped down on the front stoop.

When Eunice walked into her house, she was
greeted by the scent of cinnamon and cloves. She
dropped her backpack on the floor and flew into the

kitchen. Her dad leaned over the counter, examining an orange-colored pie. Eunice stood next to him and breathed in deeply. Pumpkin pie. One of her favorites. Maybe the day wasn't a total loss after all.

Dad tapped the side of the pie pan with his hand. The pie filling remained steady. He nodded. "No jiggle. Good." Dad kissed the top of her head. "How was the first day?"

"Terrible. Just terrible," Eunice said. "Did you make the pie for me?"

"Of course it's for you." Dad tapped her on the nose. "I'm working on a new recipe. I'm trying to make a pumpkin pie without eggs or milk."

"Why?"

"Because," he said, "it's a challenge." He leaned back to look at her. "What do you mean, terrible?"

She told him about how they had changed the rules of The Contest. "Teamwork is the key to success!" she said, and stuck her finger down her throat like she wanted to throw up. Then she told him about Ms. Hobart and her grandfather's hat, and how she had picked out the pairs one by one until finally, at the end, she got paired with the worst possible person on earth.

"Thad?" Dad said.

Eunice heaved a sigh and nodded. "Good-bye, Rainier Cruiser. You were so lovely. Now I'll never ride you, except in my dreams."

Dad burst out laughing.

Eunice was indignant. "Why are you laughing?"

"That doesn't sound like the Eunice I know. I thought maybe you were an actress on the Masquers Theater stage." Dad threw his hand up over his forehead and, in slow motion, keeled over onto the counter. His voice got unnaturally high. "My life is over! I've been paired with the most evil boy on earth! I'm doomed!"

Eunice tried to scowl but smiled in spite of herself. She socked him on the shoulder. Dad smiled. He straightened up and put his hands on her shoulders. His smile faded. "Yangs do not give up." His eyes had a hint of sadness. "Even when the worst happens, the Yangs keep going."

Eunice nodded and looked down. She knew why his eyes were sad. It was about her mother dying when Eunice was one. She didn't want to think about it. Part of her still wanted to feel sorry for herself. "I've trained for so long," she said. "I wanted to win."

Dad put his arm around her shoulder and steered her out of the kitchen. "Some things are more important than winning." He gave her a gentle push down the hall. Turning back to the kitchen, he called over his shoulder, "Like pumpkin pie!"

Eunice picked up her backpack from where she had dropped it. She pictured Thad's face with its usual smirk. But when their names had been read out loud, Thad was just as shocked as she was. For once, he hadn't made a face at her. For once, he had looked like a regular boy.

7. TETHERBALL DEATH MATCH

The next morning at school, all Eunice could think of was tetherball. There was nothing like hitting a ball round and round a pole when you're mad. When the recess bell rang, Eunice ran outside with the rest of her classmates, but Thad and Buzz had gotten to the tetherball courts first.

Eunice and Thad had managed to not speak a word to each other ever since their names were pulled out of the old straw hat. Generally, Eunice avoided matching off with Thad in any games. It always ended in name-calling, no matter who won. She wanted to avoid him, but she really needed to give something a pounding, and his line was the shortest.

Eunice had to give it to Thad. He was a good player, even at his height. Usually the best players were the tallest kids in the class. But when Thad was up against someone taller, he would jump up a little more every time he hit the ball. He made up for his deficiencies.

After a few more games, it was her turn. Eunice stepped into the circle. She and Thad were exactly the same height. He held the tetherball in his left hand. He had a gleam in his eye. She was about to say "ready" when Thad smacked the ball with his right hand.

Jerk! Eunice hit the ball back.

Thwack! Thad returned it.

The thwack of a tetherball was one of Eunice's most favorite sounds on earth. She had only one thing on her mind: winning.

She hit it high. He jumped and hit it back—hard. She hit it back just as hard.

Thwack! Thwack! Thwack! Thwack!

"C'mon!" Carson yelled from the line. "We haven't got all day!"

The first bell rang. Kids left to get in line to go back inside.

Thwack! Thwack! Thwack! Thwack!

The second bell rang. Ms. Hobart would be on the playground any minute. Eunice couldn't look away. Thad's beady eyes were focused. There was no way she was stopping.

Ms. Hobart stomped over to them. "Recess is over. Stop now."

They didn't. Ms. Hobart walked away and led the rest of the class inside. A few minutes later, she reappeared. She might as well have been invisible. Eunice wasn't going to stop until Thad stopped. Yangs did not give up.

"I'm warning you. One, two—" Without saying "three," Ms. Hobart stepped into the circle and grabbed the tetherball in midflight. Eunice and Thad were sweating like dogs. They both bent over, hands on their knees, breathing hard.

Ms. Hobart's eyes seared into them. "You'll stop when I tell you to." Eunice and Thad gave her blank looks as they sucked in gobs of air. Eunice was happy to see Thad was breathing just as hard as she was. Ms. Hobart pointed her finger at them, then toward the building. "Report to the principal's office now."

"But, Ms. Hobart—" Eunice said.

"No buts. Go!"

Eunice shot an accusing look at Thad. His eyes shot daggers back. As they shuffled slowly to the principal's office, Eunice worried that Mr. Moss would call her dad. She could deal with any kind of punishment but couldn't bear the thought of her dad's face when he saw her in the principal's office again. And his boss would not be happy if he had to leave work. She silently prayed, even though she'd never been to church.

"This is your fault," Thad muttered.

"Me? What about you?"

"You should have stopped."

"You should have!"

"I've got the worst luck, getting a witch like you for my partner."

No one was going to call her a witch and get away with it. Eunice shoved Thad with all her might, catching him off guard. He stumbled backward. His heel caught on a crack in the sidewalk and he fell down on the cement.

An elderly woman with a kind face came out of the building. "Are you okay?"

Thad got up and brushed the dust off the back of his jeans. "You saw what she did, didn't you, Mrs. Schneider?"

Mrs. Schneider fixed Eunice with a withering look. She ushered Eunice and Thad into the front office waiting area. Eunice's cheeks flamed. Nice Mrs. Schneider, the school secretary, had seen her shove Thad. Why couldn't she learn to control herself?

"I'm sorry, Mrs. Schneider," Eunice said. "But you didn't hear what he called me."

"Eunice," she said. "Name-calling is no excuse for violence."

Shoving was violence? He wouldn't have fallen if there hadn't been that crack in the sidewalk.

Mrs. Schneider went into Mr. Moss's office and closed the door. The wall that faced the waiting room was all glass, so they could both see him clearly. He was on the phone. After he hung up, he and Mrs. Schneider exchanged words. She opened the office door. "Mr. Moss will see you now."

Eunice and Thad shuffled in with their heads down, like two criminals awaiting their sentences. Mrs. Schneider closed the door behind her. Eunice's stomach had passed the stuck accordion stage; it was now tying itself into knots.

"Please sit down," Mr. Moss said. "So I hear you both love tetherball?"

"Yes, sir," Eunice and Thad said together.

"I love tetherball too. But you know, when recess is over, you have to get in line." Mr. Moss smiled. "I mean, can you imagine if everyone kept playing when the bell rang? Why, it'd be anarchy."

They both nodded. Eunice made a mental note to look up the word "anarchy."

Thad shifted in his seat. "Mr. Moss, did Mrs. Schneider tell you—"

Mr. Moss held up his hand. "She did." He turned to Eunice. "We won't tolerate violence at our school."

There was that word again. Eunice made a mental note to look up "violence" too. She wasn't convinced that shoving was included in the definition.

"Yes, sir," she said. "But you didn't hear what he called me."

"Name-calling is no excuse." Mr. Moss was no longer smiling. Eunice looked down. Guys just didn't get it. Calling a girl a witch is fighting words.

"Thad," Mr. Moss said, "are you hurt?"

Thad's face brightened. "A little."

"I'm sorry to hear that. Please see Nurse Broom after this."

Nurse Broom was a mean, ugly woman with bad teeth. Talk about a witch. Thad piped up. "Naw, that's okay. I'm fine."

Mr. Moss nodded. "Good to hear. Now, I heard from Ms. Hobart that you two are teammates for The Contest."

Eunice and Thad nodded.

"Since you're supposed to work as a team, I've got a proposition for you." Eunice's stomach un-knotted a little. "You both will be punished, since you both broke the rules. Eunice, you'll get extra punishment for breaking two rules." Mr. Moss held out his left hand, palm up. "If you choose to work as a team, your punishment will be less." He held out his right hand at a level higher than the left. "If not, it will be more."

Eunice hoped that neither involved calling her dad, but she knew better than to hold out false hope. She only hoped that Thad felt the same way about his mom getting called. Mrs. Warfield had an important job as a nurse's assistant.

"Your choices are, one, you work together after school to pick up trash every day for one week. Eunice will do an extra week. And you get to tell your parents later why you have to pick up trash." Mr. Moss paused. "Or two, I call your parents to come in right now, and you lose recess privileges for a week." Mr. Moss shifted his palms up and down, indicating choice number one or choice number two. "Which one will it be?"

"Number one," Eunice said, too quickly. She wanted to kick herself. She really had to learn to control herself. Dang, why was it always so hard with Thad around?

Thad took his sweet time thinking it over. He drummed his grubby fingers on his knee. He made semi-whistling sounds with his mouth. Eunice's stomach would be permanently knotted before he made his decision.

"I guess . . ." Thad mused. "One."

Eunice breathed again. She almost smiled but remembered where she was and kept her lips straight as a board.

"I'm glad to see you two agree." Mr. Moss smiled. "What's teamwork?"

"The key to success," Eunice and Thad said in monotone voices.

"That's right." Mr. Moss waved them out of his office. "Do a good job with the trash pickup, or I'll hear about it from Fergus."

As they walked down the hall, Eunice felt her stomach unfurl. She breathed out and wondered if Thad felt the same relief as she did. Right before they reached the classroom, she turned to him. "Thanks."

"For what?"

"For not picking number two."

Thad shrugged. It was the best interaction they'd ever had.

8. TRASH TALK

The sun blazed down as Eunice bent to pick up an old, wadded-up tissue from Soap Lake Elementary's desert dry field. Gross. Totally gross. She dropped it into a large trash bag, thankful for rubber gloves.

Thad was about ten feet away with his own trash bag. He picked up a crushed soda can. "Why are kids such slobs?"

Eunice stood up and put her hand on her hip. "Total pigs."

After four days of silent trash pickup, they were finally having a conversation. Eunice did not count Thad's statement on their first day of duty, "You're making me miss basketball practice," to which she did not reply. This last exchange was almost friendly. Barely, but it was a start.

Soon the dried-up fields of Soap Lake Elementary were clean. Eunice longed to go home, take a cool shower, and get into a fresh T-shirt and shorts. She couldn't wait to make herself a lime rickey with limes from Mr. Oliver's tree. Her mouth watered just thinking about it.

This was their last day of picking up trash together. Eunice would do trash duty on her own next week as punishment for the shoving. Even though it was hot, dirty work, Eunice was glad she had told her dad about the punishment rather than having him hear about it from Mr. Moss. After she explained, Dad nodded and said, "You need to learn to control yourself." Eunice hung her head and promised she would.

They finished picking up the last scraps of trash and recycling, and dragged their bags to the garbage bin area. A shriveled old man, tanned as brown leather and with wooly white hair, came around the corner. "Hey, kids." He took their garbage bags, tied them up, and threw them into the bins. He took their bags full of recyclables and shuffled away at a snail's pace. "Thanks for making my job easy."

Eunice and Thad watched him go. He was a nice old man, but he could barely get around anymore. "I wonder how long Fergus is going to last," muttered Thad.

"Yeah," Eunice said. Another exchange without fighting. They walked in the same direction across the school parking lot. She summoned her courage. "Are you ready for the obstacle course?"

"Why do you care?"

"Just asking."

"You think you're so hot. Miss Best Runner. Miss Best Reader. You make me sick."

It was an insult and a compliment at the same time. Eunice didn't know which way to take it. She chose the middle. "I'm not the best runner. Carson's the best."

"I wish I had him for a partner instead of you," Thad said. "Even if he is a stuck-up Goody-Two-Shoes," he added under his breath.

Eunice's heart leapt. Thad felt the same way about Carson as she did. "They're going to be hard to beat."

"Yeah." Thad kicked a rock across the parking lot. "Hard, but not impossible."

Eunice started to say something else, but they had reached Second Avenue and Thad made a sharp left without saying good-bye. He headed toward Hemlock Street. She watched him walk away, then turned right toward Buttercup.

Hemlock. What a great street for Thad to live on. Eunice had learned about the deadly plant from a science lesson in third grade. Ever since, she had often wished that Thad would go home and have a hemlock stir-fry. But his last remark had given her hope.

Hope from Thad Warfield? Eunice shook her head. It was turning out to be a year of firsts for a lot of things.

EUNICE'S LIME RICKEY
Serves two

Two tall glasses
Ice
One lime
Club soda
Sugar
Straws (optional)

1. Wash the lime. Roll it back and forth on the counter top until it gets squishy. This helps to make the lime juicy. Cut the lime in half and pick out the seeds.
2. Fill the glasses about one-third of the way with ice.
3. Squeeze one lime half into each glass and drop in. Make sure to scoop out any seeds that escape into the glasses.
4. Fill each glass with club soda.
5. Add two teaspoons of sugar to each glass and stir until the sugar melts. Taste the rickey and add more sugar if needed.
6. Sip rickey through a straw. It's especially good on hot days.

9. OVER THE WALL

A colony of butterflies had set up house in Eunice's stomach. Good thing the obstacle course was in the morning instead of in the afternoon. She wouldn't have been able to eat lunch if it had been in the afternoon on account of being too worried about puking.

Mobs of kids milled about the Lava Links Pitch-and-Putt golf course. When a whistle blew, they turned to see Mr. Moss signaling them to gather round. "Attention, contenders!"

Eunice joined the rest of her class and the other fifth grade class in front of Mr. Moss. Ms. Hobart counted heads to make sure all of her students were there. Mr. Bahr, the other fifth-grade teacher, counted heads too. Eunice spied Thad in the crowd. Ever since trash pickup had ended, she had tried talking to him again, but he had made it a point to avoid her.

Every Soap Lake Elementary student was there. As a kindergartner, Eunice thought The Contest obstacle course was the most exciting thing she had ever seen. Now she was finally competing. Standing in the crowd were her dad, Mr. Oliver, and Watson. It looked like the whole town had turned out. Her dad waved. Mr. Oliver saluted. Watson woofed. Eunice laughed and waved back.

"Okay, everyone, the course this year is pretty simple." Mr. Moss motioned to the course that lay ahead. "Simple, but not easy." He held up a clipboard with a list on it. "We've split you up into six groups of six. We can't have too many contenders on the course at one time."

Mr. Moss pointed to the start line. "You'll start here with a race around the markers you see set up on the links. Then go through the tires, one foot in each tire. Then crawl through the tunnel. After that, head to the wall. Scale it, and you're in the final stretch. Do five pull-ups on the bar, and then cross the finish line."

There were a lot of groans when Mr. Moss mentioned pull-ups. Eunice silently rejoiced. She had seen kids struggling to do pull-ups on the course back when she was in first grade. Ever since, she'd been training on the old oak tree in her backyard. They didn't have pull-ups last year or the year before, but she knew they would eventually turn up again. A few butterflies in her stomach flew away.

Mr. Moss pointed at a group of senior citizens standing at the end of the course. "We have six judges who will clock in your time as you cross the finish line. The fastest team wins the most points." Mr.

Moss blew his whistle. "Group number one! Line up!"

Eunice wished she was in group one. Instead, she was in group six. Thad was in group five. They had to wait. Eunice hated waiting.

Jenny and Callie Hernandez lined up with group one. Jenny was all smiles, wagging her ponytail, tied with a lavender ribbon, from side to side. She didn't look nervous at all. She was also wearing a lavender T-shirt and white shorts printed with lavender dots. Eunice frowned. The old Jenny wouldn't have been caught dead in that outfit. White shorts for an obstacle course? Dumbhead.

Mr. Moss blasted the air horn. They were off! Callie Hernandez led the pack. She was fast. Not as fast as Carson or Eunice, but pretty dang close. Surprisingly, Jenny was keeping up too.

The group made it through the run, the tires, and the tunnel. Then several of them hit the wall. Literally. It was straight up about ten feet and made of heavy planks of wood. Some tried to scale it but jumped back down without making it to the other side. No matter how hard she tried, Jenny couldn't get her leg up and over it. She was disqualified along with four other contenders. Callie made it over, though it cost her precious time. Sergey made it over too.

At the pull-up bar, Sergey did three quickly and then struggled, sweat pouring down his face as he tried to do another. Callie slowly but steadily did her pull-ups, the minutes ticking away. Finally, she pulled herself up one last time, dropped to the ground, and sped across the finish line. Sergey followed a minute later. Eunice pumped her fist in silence. She knew she could beat Callie's time.

Groups two, three, and four went next. Every once in a while, Eunice glanced over at Thad. He seemed to be concentrating hard on the course. She was invisible to him. Why were they even on the same team?

Then it was group five's turn. Thad and Carson were in the same group. Everyone paid more attention when they saw this, as if they all knew that this was the match to watch.

They took off at the sound of the horn. Almost immediately, Carson pulled ahead of Thad, but Thad moved quicker through the tires and the tunnel. Eunice marveled at the way he scaled the wall like a tree monkey. Then he did five pull-ups in no time at all and was across the finish line before Carson had even finished one.

Eunice whooped. She couldn't help it. Even though Thad was still the most evil boy on earth, she knew by the looks on the judges' faces that he had the best time. Now she just had to do her best, and the match was theirs.

"Last group! Group number six!"

The butterflies in Eunice's stomach returned with a vengeance. She felt like she was going to puke. She'd been waiting for this her whole life. She'd been training every day for almost four years. She had to win. She just had to.

As Eunice stretched and warmed up at the start line, someone bumped into her hard. "Watch it!" Eunice turned to wallop the kid, then realized it was Thad. He bent so close she could feel his hot breath in her ear.

"On the wall, go right." Thad shoved her a little, scowled, and walked away. He then high-fived Buzz.

The air horn sounded. Eunice took off, puzzled at Thad's advice. Go right on the wall. Go right.

Thinking about what Thad had said slowed Eunice down. Suddenly, Buzz was ahead of her. Dang it! She could hear people cheering and Watson howling. She was right behind Buzz on the tires and practically biting his heels in the tunnel. She wanted to shove him out of the way, but he was too big. She didn't notice anyone else in group six. The race was between her and her archenemy's best friend.

They got to the wall. Buzz went for the left side. Eunice went for the right.

Scrabbling with her hands, Eunice found a tiny ridge for a handhold. She stretched her right foot high and, eureka! found a little ledge, barely perceptible, that gave her just enough of a foothold to raise herself up.

Buzz was struggling. Why had Thad sent her to the right side of the wall and not his best friend?

She got over the top of the wall and jumped down, landing so hard she touched the ground with both hands. She sprang up, ran, and leapt onto the pull-up bar with Buzz right behind her.

One! Two! Three! Four! Five! She dropped to the ground and ran across the finish line. A rush of relief and adrenaline washed over her. As she bent over to catch her breath, she spied Buzz straining to finish his last pull-up. Eunice jabbed the air with her fist. Hooyeah! Take that, Buzz!

The judges did some quick calculations and passed a slip of paper to Mr. Moss. He spoke through the megaphone. "We have the winners of the first event in the One Hundredth Annual Brawn and Brains Contest. They are—Thad Warfield and Eunice Yang!"

Eunice whooped. She ran to her dad. He gave her a hug, lifting her off the ground. "Way to go, kid!" Eunice had never been happier. Mr. Oliver gave her a hug too, and Watson gave her a big sloppy lick on the face. This time she didn't mind. She would never forget this moment for as long as she lived.

Eunice looked around. Thad was watching her but looked away quickly. Then Buzz ran up to him and they exchanged the macho man hand clasp. Thad kept scanning the crowd. Then his face lit up. A woman in a hospital uniform with a full head of blonde corkscrew hair ran up and hugged him. Like mother, like son.

Mrs. Warfield was pretty. She had eyes that turned into half-moons, like Mr. Oliver's, when she smiled. She did not look like the mother of evil spawn. Eunice shook her head. How could he have come from her?

Where was Thad's dad? As if in answer to her thoughts, Mrs. Warfield bent to tell Thad something. Thad's smile vanished. He kicked the ground. Thad's mom rubbed his back as they walked away.

Eunice didn't feel sorry for Thad. She was still basking in the afterglow of winning the obstacle course. She and Thad had actually won. Maybe they could be a team after all.

10. THE TOPIC

Eunice thought Thad might be friendlier after they won the obstacle course. She was wrong. Every day he found a new way to make her miserable. Each time he did something mean, he'd catch Buzz's eye, and they'd exchange an approving nod or, if it was recess, they'd high-five. It was back to business as usual.

They say time flies when you're having fun. It should be changed to time flies when you're avoiding something. Eunice avoided talking to Thad. He avoided talking to her. They both avoided thinking about the second event in The Contest: the dreaded speech.

The obstacle course was great. The science fair would be fun. But talking in front of your classmates, teachers, and the whole dang Soap Lake community? That would be torture. Eunice had heard that more people were afraid of public speaking than they were of dying. She believed it.

Eunice pictured her face turning the color of a tomato and her eyes rolling to the back of her head. She'd faint or die right there on stage. Thad would laugh his head off. Her hope for winning The Contest started to evaporate like a glass of water in the Mojave Desert.

The days grew colder, and jack-o-lanterns began to appear on doorsteps. Eunice loved riding her bike every weekend in October and seeing bright orange heads decorating porches and windows. Even though her heart sank a little each time she rode her rickety old bike, she consoled herself by counting how many carved pumpkins there were all over town. Every weekend the count rose, and her mouth watered when she thought of all the sweets she'd collect soon.

The day before Halloween, Ms. Hobart held up a stack of yellow handouts. "Here's your topic for The Contest."

Everyone started chattering. There had been much speculation about what the topic would be. Guesses ranged from Abraham Lincoln's presidency to famous buildings to animals that had gone extinct. The class held its breath. "The topic for this year's speech is"—everyone drum-rolled their desks—"insects!"

Everyone cheered. Insects were cool! There were so many good ones to choose from.

Ms. Hobart passed out the yellow sheets. "Read the directions carefully. Remember, the speech has to be five minutes."

Eunice knew what she had to do, even though she didn't want to. When the bell rang, she sped out of class, beating Thad to Hemlock Street. Thad whistled as he sauntered down the street. He scowled when he saw her. "What do you want?"

"Are we going to work together or what?"

"Now? I've got basketball practice."

"Not now. Later, for the speech. We're supposed to work as a team."

"Just because we're a team doesn't mean we have to work together."

"That's the stupidest thing I've ever heard." Eunice's face grew hot. "If we're not supposed to work together, then why'd you help me on the obstacle course?"

Thad scowled and walked away. Eunice caught up to him and grabbed his arm. He wrenched it out of her hold, glaring at her. "I knew you'd mess up on that wall. Every kid who went for the left side messed up. Didn't you notice?"

Eunice hadn't noticed. She had been so impatient to compete that she hadn't taken the time to watch the other contenders. Thad had watched. Thad had patience. Eunice felt a twinge of envy, and she didn't like it. Not one bit.

"Aren't you excited about the topic?" Eunice said.

"Nope."

Thad started walking again. Eunice yelled after him. "Doesn't being in first place mean anything to you?"

Without turning around, Thad said, "Not if it's with you."

Eunice's stomach squeezed like an accordion. Why did Thad hate her? She had reason to hate him, starting with The Incident in first grade and all the mean things he'd said and done since then. "Why do you hate me?" she said. Thad kept walking.

"WHY DO YOU HATE ME?"

Thad must have heard her, even though he pretended not to. Without turning around, he opened the door to his house and went inside.

The accordion in Eunice's stomach burned. Yelling didn't get her the reaction that she wanted. She would have to use more drastic measures.

11. IT WORE A VEIL

Eunice loved Halloween. She loved that she could dress up as anything from a princess to an ax murderer to a tomato. She loved that people gave out candy. And she loved that it was okay to play tricks on people for one night. The whole holiday was perfect.

As she placed a black patch over her left eye, Eunice practiced a menacing sneer. She was dressed as the scariest pirate around: Blackbeard. Jenny had come over after school to help her with the costume. Anna had come too. Eunice didn't like Anna, but she had to admit the girl was good with her hands. The two of them had transformed her stick-straight jet black hair into dozens of little braids in half an hour without any snarky remarks about pirates being too "fourth grade."

Eunice tied a red kerchief around her head and surveyed herself in the mirror—black full-length cape, white pirate shirt with long poufy sleeves, black jeans rolled up to her knees, red-and-black-striped tights, and black boots. She picked up her plastic saber and brandished it in the air. "Arrr, matey!" she growled.

"Whoa," Dad said, backing up a few steps. "You get scarier every year."

Eunice pointed her saber at Dad. "Get outta my way or yer walkin' the plank."

Dad snapped photos as Eunice brandished her way out of her room and down the hall. He yelled after her, "Remember, nine thirty at the Lucky Dragon!"

"Arrr!" Eunice yelled back, swinging her pillowcase decorated with skulls over her shoulder and dashing out the door. Meeting at the Lucky Dragon at the end of the night was a Yang tradition. Once she was old enough to trick-or-treat on her own, Eunice would meet her dad just as he was getting off work, and they would walk home together.

The rolls of toilet paper hidden in her pillowcase bounced against Eunice's back as she sped to Main and Elder to meet Jenny and Anna. Kids were already trick-or-treating up and down the street by the time she got there. It was just getting dark. Jenny was dressed as Cinderella. Anna was Juliet from *Romeo and Juliet*. Eunice thought they were both super boring, but they had helped her with her hair. "Cool costumes," she said.

"Thanks." They both smiled widely and twirled around, showing off their skirts.

Sergey was dressed as a surgeon with rubber gloves and blood-stained scrubs. He was family friends with Anna. Eunice eyed his stains. "Nice blood, doc."

"Beet juice," he beamed. He examined her costume. "Blackbeard, eh?" He nodded with approval. "Cool saber."

Not bad for a boy who wasn't allowed to read wizarding books. Why did Sergey and Anna's parents approve of Halloween? If their kids couldn't read books about witchcraft, then why was it okay to celebrate a holiday filled with witches, goblins, and ghosts? Another wacky grown-up rule.

A tall, brawny boy dressed as a medieval knight stood near a lamppost brandishing his plastic sword and stabbing it into imaginary opponents. Sergey jerked his thumb in the boy's direction. "My cousin Olaf. He's from Moses Lake." He called out, "This is Eunice!" Olaf looked at her and grunted.

Eunice didn't mind having the two boys along, even though Jenny and Anna were tossing their hair like mad and giggling with each other. It helped to have a mixed group because they would be targeted less by high schoolers who loved to throw water balloons as they sped by in their cars. Last year, trick-or-treating with an all-girl group, Eunice and Jenny were soaked to the bone by the time they got home.

Anna batted her eyelashes at Olaf. Dumbhead and dumbhead. Eunice stopped herself from putting her finger down her throat. "Let's go," she said, holding her sword aloft and moving down the street.

It was tradition to start trick-or-treating at all the stores and restaurants on Main Avenue, and then head to the neighborhood houses. It was also tradition for all the stores and restaurants to give out weird, inedible treats. When they got to Masquers Theater, Watson bounded out of nowhere, jumped on Eunice, and licked her nose. He was wearing a little houndstooth cape around his neck. Eunice grimaced and wiped the slobber off her nose with the edge of her cape.

Mr. Oliver appeared, wearing a funny hat and a long wooly trench coat, and clenching a pipe in his teeth. He carried a large bowl filled with red and blue squishy balls that looked like they were made out of Jell-O.

"Hey, Sherlock," Eunice said. "Hey, Dr. Watson." She petted the bloodhound, who nudged her with his head, then left to snuffle the other kids. Anna screamed and scampered away. "He won't bite," Eunice said. "He'll just drool all over you."

"Exactly, my dear," Mr. Oliver said, winking at Eunice.

Sergey and Jenny laughed and reached out their hands for Watson to sniff before they patted him. Anna made a face and stood behind Olaf. Olaf grunted.

The kids gathered around Mr. Oliver and dug their hands into the bowl.

"Look," said Sergey. "It goes with my costume." He held a ball right in front of Eunice's face and squeezed. It made a sickening squishy sound. Hoo-yeah! Eunice grabbed one and squeezed it in Jenny's face. Jenny squealed with delight and grabbed one for herself. "Thanks," they called back to Mr. Oliver and Watson as they hurried to their next destination.

By the time they got to the end of Main Avenue, Eunice's pillowcase was loaded down with a brain ball, two decks of cards, a red rubber clown nose, a sticky spider that could climb down walls, a mini lava lamp keychain, a plastic dragon, a foam rocket, and several rubber snakes. As they made the rounds through the neighborhood, their bags got heavier and heavier with mini candy bars, suckers, sour gumballs, and other sweet treats. Gummy bears were Eunice's favorite and she already had three little bags of them. At the end of the night, Eunice would separate her loot into piles and count up how much she had of each type of candy. She loved that part of Halloween.

The night was turning out better than she thought it would. Even Jenny seemed more like her old self once they got going. They were near Buttercup Street when Olaf finally uttered the first word he'd said all night. "Whoa," he said, his mouth hanging open. Eunice followed his eyes to see Mrs. Lebowitz's place completely covered in toilet paper. It looked like a giant marshmallow. A group of boys was putting on the finishing touches.

"Know 'em?" Eunice whispered to Sergey.

Sergey looked them up and down. "Ephrata," he said. "I'm pretty sure."

Dang Ephrata kids. Why couldn't they TP their own town? Something sparked in Eunice's stomach. She walked into the front yard. "You know whose house this is?"

"Some old bat," said a boy with sandy brown hair falling into his eyes. He wore ripped clothes and had fake blood all over his mouth and chin.

"She's not just some old bat. She's the Black Widow."

"Ooh, I'm scared." The boy threw up his hands in mock terror. His gang gathered around him. Jenny,

Anna, Sergey, and Olaf walked up and stood behind Eunice. Five against five. Eunice started to sweat.

"She's a witch, you know," Eunice warned.

The gang doubled over, laughing. "Did you hear that?" they asked each other. "She's a witch!" They laughed like it was the funniest thing in the world.

The boys snickered as they slowly surrounded Eunice and her group. Anna looked nervous. Sergey and Olaf puffed out their chests and stretched to their full height. Eunice and Jenny exchanged glances. Jenny had the same look she had had when they were in the first-grade mud fight. Good old Jenny. Eunice felt a little better—but only a little. She had thought they might get pelted with water balloons on Halloween, but she had never thought they'd get beat up by a bunch of Ephrata kids.

Eunice tried again. "She'll put a curse on you."

"Oh no," Zombie Boy said. "I want my mommy!"

Eunice was glad to have a saber, even if it was only plastic. She could poke someone in the eye if she had to. Zombie Boy got so close to her she could smell his stinky breath. She was about to stab him and yell "Run!" at the top of her lungs when suddenly a bloodcurdling scream came from inside the house.

Everyone spun around in time to see something dressed in a tattered floor-length black lace dress with long ripped sleeves coming toward them. A black headpiece and veil completely covered its head and sickly white face. Its arms stretched out in front as it lurched toward them. Blood dripped from its mouth. "Come here," it said in a voice that made Eunice's hair stand on end. "Come to me."

The boys took off faster than a pack of cheetahs. Not far behind were Jenny, Anna, Sergey, and Olaf. Cowards! Eunice scowled at their retreating figures, but she knew she'd have been right with them if all the blood hadn't drained out of her legs.

The black figure stopped in front of Eunice. Eunice sucked in her breath and felt her legs wobble. One of its arms lifted the veil slightly to reveal a wrinkled face covered with a thick layer of green makeup and fake blood. Eunice exhaled as she recognized Mrs. Lebowitz in the pale moonlight.

"The one and only Black Widow," she said.

Eunice winced. "I'm sorry, Mrs. Lebowitz. I was just trying to—"

Mrs. Lebowitz waved her off like an errant fly and dropped her veil over her face. "I know what you kids call me," she said. "I didn't just fall off the turnip truck, you know." She looked up and down the street.

"Such a shame no one ever trick-or-treats at my door anymore." She shuffled back toward her house. "I love dressing up for the occasion—and I give out the best treats."

The Black Widow loved Halloween? She felt the blood coming back into her legs. What kind of treats?

Eunice wobbled a bit as she followed Mrs. Lebowitz up the walk and onto the porch. Mrs. Lebowitz reached through the door and picked up a bowl. "I always order a supply in case anyone comes," she said with a sigh, "but no one ever does."

The bowl was filled with individually wrapped gummy tarantulas the size of Eunice's palm. They were the most awesome candies she'd ever seen. Mrs. Lebowitz dumped the contents of the bowl into Eunice's pillowcase.

"Thanks," Eunice said. She didn't know what else to say. She turned and walked down the steps.

When Eunice got to the gate, she looked back over her shoulder. Mrs. Lebowitz was still standing there. If she hadn't know it was her, she'd be scared out of her gourd. Eunice smiled and waved. She could have sworn that the Black Widow smiled back, but it was too hard to tell through the veil.

12. THE GIFT

The day after Halloween, Eunice got up at six o'clock to help her dad take all the toilet paper off Mrs. Lebowitz's house and front yard. Dad said she would get a special dinner that night if she helped, but deep down Eunice knew she would have done it even if he hadn't offered. She didn't like the idea of Mrs. Lebowitz looking out her window and seeing all that TP, soggy and saggy with dew. Plus Mrs. Lebowitz couldn't look for spiders if the bushes were covered with toilet paper.

She didn't know if it was the Halloween incident with Mrs. Lebowitz or the gummy tarantulas that she was eating every day, but Eunice became obsessed with spiders. She had checked out a book on spiders from the school library and read about them in her spare time.

On Friday, Ms. Hobart gave the class time to split into their contest teams to work on their speeches. During the hour, she walked around the room and monitored whether team members were working together. Eunice was glad Ms. Hobart was so strict. Without her goading them on, Eunice and Thad would never have gotten anything done.

Eunice showed her book to Thad, opening to a page with a photo of a black spider with an hourglass-shaped red marking. "How about doing our speech on the black widow?"

Thad glanced at it. "How about spiders in general?"

Eunice shook her head. "The winning speeches are always on one thing. Like last year when Marcus Mihalyo did his on the African gray parrot."

Thad made a face at her and went back to flipping through his book.

Eunice whispered, "You may not care, but I want to win."

"You just want that stupid bike."

"The Rainier Cruiser is not stupid!"

Ms. Hobart appeared at their side. "Everything okay here?"

"Yes, Ms. Hobart," they both muttered.

"Good," Ms. Hobart said. "Back to work."

Thad waited until Ms. Hobart was out of earshot. "Why don't you ask your daddy to buy that stupid bike for you?"

"At least I have a dad."

"I have a dad!"

Ms. Hobart shot a look in their direction. Thad bent his head low. "He's looking for a job," he said under his breath, his face flushing. "And when he gets one, we'll be together, and he's going to buy me any bike I want."

Eunice could tell she wasn't going to get anywhere with Thad. She was getting more and more frustrated by the minute. Then it dawned on her. Why work with him at all? She leaned toward him. "I'll write the speech. You just have to read the parts that are yours." Thad shrugged and went back to thumbing through his book. Dumbhead. No wonder people said "if you want something done right, do it yourself."

November passed so quickly, Eunice almost forgot about Thanksgiving until Ms. Hobart had the class write essays about what they were grateful for. Eunice wrote about being grateful for her dad, Mr. Oliver, Watson, and her dad's pumpkin pie. At the last minute, she added Mrs. Lebowitz and the gummy tarantulas.

On Thanksgiving Day, Eunice, Dad, and Mr. Oliver bundled up in their heavy coats, scarves, hats, and boots, and slogged through the snow to the high school gym for the town potluck. Traditionally, anyone in Soap Lake who didn't have a family reunion to go to was welcome. Some had reunions to go to but they still came to the potluck. Maybe it was because of her dad's famous pumpkin pies.

After the potluck, Dad gave Eunice a bag of leftovers and an egg- and dairy-free pumpkin pie that he had baked. "Could you take these to Mrs. Lebowitz?"

"Can you come with me?" Eunice asked.

"You can handle it, kid."

Sometimes Eunice didn't understand her dad. But she did as he said and took the pie and leftovers next door. Mrs. Lebowitz answered the door wearing her usual black outfit, but this time she had a wooly gray scarf wrapped around her neck and lower face. It was the most color Eunice had ever seen her wear, other than her pink-and-black-striped socks. It looked very scratchy. How could she stand wearing it? She held out the bundle and the pie. "Happy Thanksgiving."

"Whafppy Fanksgiving." Mrs. Lebowitz unwound her scarf. "Sorry, I've got a terrible cold," she said, and sneezed into her arm.

"Are you okay?"

"I'll be fine," Mrs. Lebowitz said, holding up the pie, "once I eat lots of your dad's pie." She turned to walk away with the food but said over her shoulder, "Wait just a minute." She came back carrying a thick black leather-bound book and handed it to Eunice.

Eunice nearly dropped it, it was so heavy. "What is it?"

Mrs. Lebowitz started sneezing her head off. She shooed Eunice off the porch. "Go, go. I don't want you to catch this."

"Thanks," Eunice said. She turned to go home, but not before peeking inside the book. Her heart leapt. It was an entire book on spiders! There was even a whole chapter dedicated to the black widow. After trudging through the snow to get home, she kicked off her boots and ran to the kitchen. "Look what Mrs. Lebowitz gave me!"

Dad just smiled.

The days after Thanksgiving sped by. The book that Mrs. Lebowitz had given her was ten times better than the one she had checked out from the library. Every Friday in class, Eunice and Thad pretended they were working together on their speech. Eunice would show Thad what she had written, and he would shrug or grunt. Even though she was doing all the work and it made her mad when she thought about it, she preferred it over arguing with him.

The winter holiday arrived, giving Eunice the two weeks off from school—and from Thad. On the first Monday morning of the break, Eunice and her dad drove out to a tree farm. They cut down a tree and tied it to the top of their car. Once home, they made popcorn and fresh cranberry chains and hung them over the tree's branches. Dad brought out a box of homemade ornaments from the hall closet. Eunice decorated the lower branches while Dad hung ornaments on the higher ones. Over lunch they munched sandwiches and popcorn and admired their handiwork.

"Awesome tree, kid," Dad said.

"Totally awesome," Eunice said, her mouth full of popcorn.

After lunch, Eunice went to her room, opened her sock drawer, and pulled out a snowman made of walnuts glued together, painted white, and wearing a little black felt hat. She wrapped it in tissue paper and placed it under the tree. Dad picked it up and shook it.

"What could it be?"

Eunice laughed. He knew it was an ornament. Every year they exchanged homemade ornaments instead of buying Christmas presents. They used their money instead to buy gifts for Eunice's teacher, Dad's boss and coworkers, and their neighbors. Eunice ran to her room, grabbed her wallet, and headed to the front door. "Let's go! Let's go!"

"Okay, okay," Dad laughed. "Let me get my

shoes."

Eunice counted her money again on the ride over to the grocery store in Ephrata. She had just enough to buy gifts for Watson, Mr. Oliver, and Ms. Hobart, with enough left over to get the cherry bike bell from Bob's Bicycle Shop. She buzzed with excitement.

At the store, Dad and Eunice each got their own cart. "Synchronize watches," Dad said. They checked to make sure they had the same time. Christmas shopping was a timed contest every year. "Whoever gets to the TP aisle first wins. Ready?"

"Go!" said Eunice as she sped off, her cart wheels spinning wildly. She went straight for the dog food aisle and picked out a box of dog treats that looked like bacon. Next was the jelly aisle. Mr. Oliver liked his tea and scones, and he had talked about eating gooseberries as a child. What ho! Eunice found a jar of gooseberry jam and placed it in her cart. Next was the candy aisle, where she selected a tin of Ms. Hobart's favorite toffee candy.

She was going to win! Eunice veered her way to the paper goods aisle, almost running over a woman examining cans of beans, when she saw a display of scarves and hats near the checkout stands. She screeched to a halt. One long scarf had pink and black stripes, just like Mrs. Lebowitz's socks. She reached out to touch it; it was as soft as a bunny. She looked at the price tag. It would eat up the rest of her savings. Mrs. Lebowitz didn't even celebrate Christmas. Dad had already made her butter cookies for Hanukkah. She didn't need another present, did she?

Eunice got to the toilet paper aisle right as Dad came screeching around the corner with his cart. Eunice whooped and pumped her fist. "I won!"

As they headed to the cashier, they passed by the scarves again. Eunice thought about Mrs. Lebowitz's awful scratchy-looking gray scarf. She thought about the spider book and how helpful it had been. And she thought about the gummy tarantulas.

They were almost through checking out when Eunice took off. The cashier raised her eyebrows. Dad smiled and shrugged his shoulders.

Eunice grabbed the pink-and-black-striped scarf and zipped back in line. "Excuse me," she said, squeezing by several annoyed shoppers. "Merry Christmas."

"Who's that for?" Dad asked.

"Someone," Eunice said. Dad looked at her expectantly, but Eunice just smiled. For once she didn't feel like explaining or sharing with her father.

On Christmas morning, after Eunice and her dad opened their gifts—ornaments, of course—they went next door to visit Mr. Oliver and Watson. Mr. Oliver fawned over Eunice's jam and her dad's scones. Watson drooled over the bacon treats and gobbled half the box before Mr. Oliver put them away. And as they did every year, they all sat down for a breakfast of tea, scones, cookies, jam, and sandwiches.

An hour later, Eunice and her dad trudged back home, stuffed full of good food and tea. While her dad took a nap in front of the fireplace, Eunice got the wrapped-up scarf from her closet and walked next door to Mrs. Lebowitz's house. She tiptoed to the front door and placed the gift on the doorstep. The porch creaked as she left.

The curtains in the upstairs window stirred. A wrinkled forehead and two eyes appeared, squinting into the bright winter morning just as Eunice jumped, light as a rabbit, from the front porch and into the fresh snow.

13. THE SPEECH

Suddenly, it was January. Thad bugged her about the speech every day. "I'll get it done," Eunice snapped, "with no help from you."

The last week before the speech competition, Eunice worked on her notes every day after school. She wrote the speech from the black widow's point of view. She wrote about how her bite can kill a human. She described how she would catch a "husband," and then kill him so she'd have the strength to lay her eggs and feed her baby spiders. At the end she revealed what she was. It was pretty clever.

Eunice gave the speech to Thad on Friday during their last work time together. "Be ready on Monday."

"Don't worry about me," Thad said, snatching it away from her.

That weekend, Eunice went over the speech again. She read it aloud with Dad. Some parts didn't sound right. She moved around the paragraphs and rewrote a few lines here and there. On Sunday night she printed out two new copies, one for her and one for Thad.

Monday morning came. Eunice was anxious to get the speech over and done with. If Thad read his part according to plan, they might have a shot at winning first or second place. Before class, Eunice found Thad shooting hoops on the basketball court. She handed him the revised speech. "I made a few changes."

"Why'd you change it? You didn't ask me."

"I didn't have to ask you. Who wrote this whole thing, huh?"

"You should have told me."

Eunice was livid. How dare he say that? She was ready to sock him. "Just read it."

"But I can't—"

Eunice walked away before he could say more. If she stayed, she would end up in Mr. Moss's office again.

The speeches were scheduled right after roll call and the pledge of allegiance. The contest committee knew none of the fifth graders would be able to sit through class if they were thinking about their speeches. They walked into the gym where the rest of the school and the whole Soap Lake community were waiting. Butterflies filled Eunice's stomach, just like the day of the obstacle course. She tried to focus on her breathing. She was so focused that she didn't even look in the stands for her dad.

Mr. Moss stood behind the podium. "Welcome to the second event of the One Hundredth Annual Brawn and Brains Contest. Let's get right to it. Presenters will be picked at random." He reached into a hat and pulled out a slip of paper. "The first team is—Eunice Yang and Thad Warfield!"

Eunice was shaking in her high-tops, terrified and relieved at the same time. For good luck, she had worn them instead of her winter boots, though now her feet were freezing. She glanced at Thad as they walked up to the podium together. His face was paler than usual. Her heart beat so fast, she thought she might faint.

Eunice and Thad clutched their speeches. Mr. Moss held up a stopwatch. "Remember, you have five minutes." He clicked the button and signaled for them to start.

Eunice began. "Let me begin by telling you where I live. I live in the United States, in Southern Europe, and Australia . . ."

As she read, Eunice looked up every once in a while. She remembered that tip from Ms. Hobart. Thad was shifting his weight from one side to the other. It was making her nervous. She reached the end of her part and moved over so Thad could step up to the microphone. He didn't say anything. She whispered, "Go, Thad."

Thad leaned into the mic and tapped it. "Is this thing on?" The audience laughed. Mr. Moss smiled and elbowed Jerry, the tech guy. Eunice smiled nervously. Maybe Thad was just getting warmed up. "I guess it's on." He cleared his throat. He looked down at his speech. Then he looked out into the audience for what seemed like an eternity. "Let me tell you what I like to eat. Ladies, if you're squeamish, you might want to cover your ears."

Eunice panicked. Thad wasn't supposed to talk about that part. She was. He went on and on about the black widow killing her husband. "Then I bite into him like a big, juicy hamburger! Mmmmm!" Everyone laughed.

Thad was going off-script. He was ruining the whole thing. Eunice edged closer to him and motioned at the speech behind the podium so no one else could see. "You're supposed to say this," she hissed.

Thad ignored her. He went on and on, making up stuff as he went along. He was hamming it up like a cheesy game show host. Then he skipped over Eunice's next part and went right to the end. "And if you haven't guessed by now, I am—" Thad motioned for Eunice to take the mic.

Eunice gave him a look that said the black widow's husband wasn't the only one who was going to die. Thad grinned hard at her. "C'mon, Eunice," Thad said. "Say what you are."

Eunice leaned into the mic. "I am the black widow spider."

Mr. Moss held up his hand and clicked the stopwatch. Everyone clapped, but Eunice didn't hear them. She walked zombie-like back to her seat. All she could see was red. Thad had ruined her speech. She didn't listen to any of the other speeches. Suddenly, the last team had finished and everyone was clapping.

The judges deliberated, then passed a slip of paper to Mr. Moss. He went up to the podium. "The judges have made their decision." Mr. Moss waved for the drum roll made by everyone's stomping feet on the bleachers. "Let's hear it for them! The winners of the Brawn and Brains speech competition are— Carson and Callie Hernandez!" More clapping and cheering. "The second place winners are—Jules West and Marty Patterson!"

Eunice's heart sank into her stomach. The speech was worth more points than the obstacle course. The twins were now in first place. The nerds were second. And Eunice and Thad had dropped to third. At the rate they were going, she had no chance of winning. And it was all Thad's fault.

14. A PROMISE FULFILLED

Eunice avoided her dad and Mr. Oliver. She knew if she talked to them, she'd start crying. She waved at them weakly and headed back to class.

Thad and Buzz high-fived each other right in front of her as they walked out of the gym. Thad was grinning like the Cheshire Cat. Eunice was stunned. Her insides were burning up and her mouth had a weird taste like hot, rancid metal.

She would make that boy pay. Absolutely, she would make him pay.

The rest of the day sped by. Eunice couldn't eat lunch. All afternoon, her empty stomach bubbled and gurgled. By the end of the day, she was sure her stomach was eating itself. When the bell rang, she followed Thad and Buzz out the door.

"Later," Thad said to Buzz as they parted ways at the corner of Gingko and Second Avenue. Thad was headed for the basketball court. Eunice had other plans for him.

She caught up to Thad. "Hey."

Thad stopped and turned. When he saw it was her, he turned away and kept walking. Eunice ran up and tapped his shoulder. "I'm talking to you."

"What do you want?"

"Why'd you mess up the speech?"

"What are you talking about? I messed up the speech?" Thad said. "I *saved* the speech. You should be grateful."

"Are you nuts?" The rage coursing through her could have electrocuted a murderer. "You *ruined* it. You made fools out of us both. And now we're in third place!" Tears rolled down her face, which made her angrier. She didn't want to cry in front of Thad.

"I made a fool out of *you*?" Thad shook his head in disbelief. "You're so full of yourself!" He leaned in so close to Eunice she could feel his hot breath on her face. He tapped her temple twice with his finger. "Get this through your thick skull. You're never— EVER—going to get that stupid bike."

"Don't you touch me!" Eunice's heart pounded like it might explode.

Thad backed off and flapped his hands at her like he was shooing a stray cat. "Go home to Daddy, Eun-i-cycle. Maybe he can order you a bike from China."

"Don't you talk about my dad!" Eunice screamed. Before she knew it, she lunged forward and shot her right arm out. Her fist connected with Thad's eye with a resounding smack. She knew the

90

sound could not have been that loud, but to her, it was deafening. For a minute, there was complete silence.

When her hearing came back, she heard a robin singing in a tree overhead. The knuckles on her right hand throbbed with pain. Eunice looked at Thad. He held his hand over his left eye. His mouth hung open.

Then something happened that Eunice thought would never happen. Ever. Thad Warfield cried, right in front of her. He did not make a sound but tears rolled down his cheeks.

Eunice had always wanted to hit Thad and hit him good. She hadn't thought about what she would feel like after she did it. And now she knew. She felt lower than dirt.

For what seemed like forever, they just stared at each other. Then Eunice pointed to her face and closed her eyes. "Hit me," she said. "Then we'll be even."

Eunice braced herself, but nothing happened.

When she opened her eyes, Thad was gone.

15. DREAD AND CHOW MEIN

When Eunice got home, the smell of chicken chow mein greeted her like an old friend. It was her favorite meal. But Eunice's stomach was tied in a knot, despite the homey, tantalizing smell. She ran to her bedroom and flung herself on the bed.

Dad knocked on her door and popped his head in. "Where's my number one speech writer?"

His smile faded when he saw Eunice's red, tear-stained face. He sat down on the bed, his brow furrowed. Eunice cried even more.

"It wasn't that bad." Dad rubbed her back. "Thad didn't follow your script, but it still turned out okay."

"It isn't that." Her voice gurgled like she was underwater. "It's what I did after."

In a mad rush, she told her dad what had happened. How Thad had acted like he was king of the world. How proud he was of what he had done. How she had followed him after school and the argument they'd had. What Thad had said right before she hit him.

"You finally got what you wanted," Dad said. "You got back at Thad. Are you satisfied now?"

Eunice shook her head. She wanted to die. Dad put his hands on her shoulders and looked her in the eye. "What are you going to do?"

"I don't know," Eunice blubbered through her tears.

Dad held her gaze, making her cry even more. "What would you want Thad to do if he had hit you instead?"

Eunice knew then what she had to do.

It was raining as they walked over to Thad's house. Her dad covered them both with a big umbrella. Eunice carried a covered plastic tub with a dish towel wrapped around it. Her high-tops were getting soaked by the rain. They felt heavy as cement. She put one foot in front of the other and somehow made herself move.

When they got to Thad's house, her dad pressed the doorbell. A woman in nursing scrubs answered the door. "Hi, Frances," Dad said.

"Hi, Joe."

Mrs. Warfield looked so nice standing there in her pastel uniform. Eunice looked up at her dad, and he gave her an encouraging nod. She swallowed the huge lump in her throat. "Can I talk to Thad?" she squeaked.

"Come in."

Mrs. Warfield opened the door wide and ushered them in. Eunice handed her the tub, removing the towel. Dad coughed uncomfortably. "We thought you might like some chicken chow mein."

"It smells wonderful. Thank you."

Mrs. Warfield took the tub into the kitchen. Returning, she took Eunice by the shoulder and led her down the hall. The farther down the hall they walked, the more Eunice's heart pounded. She wanted to run away. She wanted to go home.

They got to Thad's door. Mrs. Warfield knocked softly. "Thad, Eunice is here. She wants to talk to you. May she come in?"

A muffled "whatever" came through the door.

Mrs. Warfield went in first. Eunice followed. Mrs. Warfield put her hand on Thad's shoulder and whispered, "Remember what we talked about." Then she left.

Thad lay on his bed with an ice pack on his eye, a basketball in his hands. "What do you want?"

Eunice shifted her gaze to the poster of the Chicago Bulls basketball team on the wall above his head. She couldn't look at him. She could barely breathe. "I'm sorry." Tears welled up in her eyes. "Really sorry."

Thad looked away from her and started throwing the ball in the air and catching it. Up and back. Up and back. This went on for what seemed like hours. "Okay." His voice was thick.

Eunice turned to leave. When she got to the door, she heard a small voice behind her say, "I'm sorry too."

Tears rolled silently down her face. Without turning around, Eunice said, "I'll understand if you want to forfeit—if you don't want to work with me anymore."

Silence.

Eunice left the room, closing the door behind her. She had thought she would feel better. She was wrong.

JOE'S CHICKEN CHOW MEIN
Serves four

Marinade:
2 tablespoons soy sauce
1 tablespoon Chinese rice wine
¼ teaspoon black pepper
2 heaping teaspoons cornstarch

Chow Mein:
2 boneless, skinless chicken breasts (about 1 pound)
1 pound dried Chinese noodles or spaghetti
2 teaspoons sesame oil
4 large carrots, peeled and cut into long matchsticks
½ of a cabbage, cut into long, thin slivers
2 large cloves of garlic, peeled and cut into 4 pieces
Fresh ginger, peeled and cut into 4 thick quarter-sized
    pieces
4 green onions, green parts only, cut on the diagonal
    into half-inch pieces
Vegetable oil
Soy sauce
Salt

1. Wash the chicken, pat it dry with paper towels,
    then cut it into 1- to 2-inch bite-sized pieces.
    Place the pieces into a bowl. Add the marinade
    ingredients and mix to combine.
2. Bring a large pot of water to a boil. Add the
    noodles and boil until they are tender but still

firm. Follow the package instructions. When cooked, drain the noodles, rinse with cold water, drain again, and place into a large bowl. Toss with the sesame oil to keep the noodles from sticking together.

3. In a wok, heat 2 tablespoons oil over high heat. If you don't have a wok, use a large frying pan. When the oil is hot, add the sliced garlic and ginger. Stir-fry until aromatic, about 30 seconds. Add the chicken. Stir-fry until the chicken turns white and is cooked through. Remove and place in a large bowl. Separate the ginger and garlic from the chicken and discard (or compost).

5. Heat 2 tablespoons of oil in the wok. When the oil is hot, add the carrots. Stir-fry until just half crisp. Add the cabbage. Sprinkle with 2 pinches of salt. Stir-fry for about 5 minutes. Add the green onion and stir-fry for 1 minute. Transfer to a large bowl.

6. Heat 1 to 2 tablespoons of oil in the wok. When the oil is hot, add the noodles. Stir-fry quickly, tossing and coating the noodles in oil. Add the cooked chicken and vegetables. Toss to combine and heat through, about 8 to 10 minutes.

7. Taste the chow mein and add a little salt or soy sauce if needed. Remember, it's better to use too little seasoning than too much! Serve in small bowls and enjoy.

16. THE HYPOTHESIS

That night, Eunice dreamt that she showed up to school in her pajamas. Thad was there with his black eye. Mr. Moss was with him. Thad pointed at her and said, "She did it!" Mr. Moss pointed at her, and then pointed at the door. Eunice was expelled. She woke up in a cold sweat.

In the morning, Eunice avoided the playground. In class, she quietly slipped into her seat and looked down at her desk. Thad had said he was sorry too, but she still didn't know where that left them. She steeled herself for the call that would come from the principal's office any minute.

Thad waltzed in right before the bell rang. Ms. Hobart looked at him in alarm, which caused the whole class to turn and stare at him—everyone except Eunice. Ms. Hobart was struggling. Should she ask him about his eye? Who gave it to him? What if it was his mom or dad? That's what some kids might have been thinking. They stared at him, then turned away out of respect.

Eunice snuck a look at Thad during class when he wasn't looking. His eye had turned a glorious shade of purple and navy blue. If she hadn't been so racked with anxiety about getting expelled, she would have stared longer. It was odd seeing a ten-year-old with such a shiner. Had she really done that?

The morning passed without a single phone call. Eunice almost exhaled but thought that Thad might still tell Ms. Hobart or Mr. Moss. Or Mrs. Warfield might call Mr. Moss this afternoon. There was still time for her to get kicked out of school.

At lunch, Eunice choked down her sandwich. She halfheartedly went out to the blacktop. She thought maybe a game of tetherball would lift her spirits or maybe some four square. Jenny and Anna were playing hopscotch. She wished she could tell Jenny—anybody really—about what had happened. Her heart weighed as heavy as lead.

Then Eunice heard a commotion on the basketball court. She walked by to see what was going on. Thad was in the middle of a group of boys yelping and crowing with delight. She tried to pretend she wasn't listening but nobody was paying attention to her. They were all too busy listening to Thad talk about who had given him the black eye. He claimed that it was a seventh grader from Ephrata Middle School who was at least a foot taller and thirty pounds heavier. "I didn't have much of a chance."

Thad shrugged. "But I got some good punches in."
The boys listened, spellbound.

Eunice was so relieved that she almost laughed out loud. She wanted to thank Thad for not telling, but she knew not to interrupt his story. Instead, she went to stand in line for tetherball.

Back in class, Ms. Hobart announced that everyone was to report to the science room for the next phase of The Contest. Relief left Eunice in one breath. Even though Thad hadn't snitched on her, he could still forfeit The Contest. He still might be mad at her. And really, she couldn't blame him.

Eunice walked with her classmates to the science room. Everyone was excited and chattering like chipmunks about the projects they were going to do.

Ms. Hobart wrote *hypothesis* on the chalk board. She turned to the class. "Does anyone know what the word hypothesis means?"

Marty and Jules shot their hands up in the air. Of course the nerds knew.

"Yes, Jules?"

"A hypothesis is a temporary explanation for a scientific problem that can be tested by research or investigation," Jules rattled off like he was spelling his name. Jules and Marty low-fived each other. What nerds.

"Excellent," beamed Ms. Hobart. "That's exactly right. And today we're going to get in our teams and brainstorm some hypotheses that you might want to investigate for the science fair."

Everyone shuffled their seats until they were all in their teams. Thad didn't move, so Eunice went to sit at his table. They avoided eye contact.

"Your homework for next week's science class is to write up three hypotheses that you might want to test for your project."

Some students looked panicky. Ms. Hobart held her hand up. "You don't have to choose which one you're going to do. You just have to come up with some ideas. That's what brainstorming is. The science fair isn't until May. You still have three months to prepare."

The panicked students relaxed, even though they knew three months really meant three weeks or even one week. They were all procrastinators. Well, except for the nerds. Marty was already scribbling on a notepad. He and Jules would have no problem coming up with three, four, or fifteen hypotheses.

Eunice hadn't talked to Thad since the fight. She had successfully avoided the topic of The Contest all together. But they couldn't hide from it any longer. "Thad, I've been thinking—"

"Yeah, me too," Thad said, rubbing his chin. "I think we should make a volcano."

Eunice blinked in surprise. "You're in?"

"Yeah, I'm in," Thad scoffed. "I'm no quitter, you know."

Eunice almost laughed, thinking of what Dad had told her. *Yangs don't quit.* Apparently Warfields don't either. She smiled.

Thad scowled. "Wipe that smile off your face, Eun-i-cycle. We've got to hypothesize."

17. WATSON TO THE RESCUE

Friday mornings were reserved for working on the science project. Ms. Hobart wanted a topic and plan in one week. Eunice and Thad were still debating their hypothesis. Thad wanted to make an exploding volcano and experiment to see which materials would make the biggest explosion. Eunice wanted to do a report on why octopuses changed colors because the octopus was one of her favorite sea animals. They went round and round.

As the minutes ticked toward the end of the school day, Eunice got a crazy idea. She was desperate to get back on track in The Contest. Because the science fair was worth more points than the previous two events, they could still win. She caught up with Thad right after the bell rang. "You want to come over and work on the science project?"

Thad frowned. "To your house?"

"Yeah, to my house." Where else did he think she meant?

"I don't know."

"My dad makes great snacks." She had to entice him somehow.

Thad thought about it a moment. "Okay."

Eunice felt strange walking with Thad to her house. Usually she was tailing him to his. This time he was going to see where she lived.

As they walked past Mr. Oliver's place, Watson bounded off the front stoop, put his front paws on the boxwoods, and woofed in greeting. Eunice went to pet him. "Hey, Watson," she said. Watson lurched forward and gave her a big sloppy lick right on the mouth. Eunice made a face. "Eww, dog germs!"

"Watson!" called Mr. Oliver from the window. "Leave Eunice alone, old boy!" Watson went back to the front stoop and plopped down.

Eunice wiped her face with her sleeve. Thad laughed. "I wonder which is dirtier, his mouth or yours?"

A light bulb went off in Eunice's head. "Thad, you're a genius!"

"Hey, kid." Her dad smiled as Eunice entered through the back door. He raised his eyebrows when he saw who was behind her. Eunice raised her eyebrows back at him.

"Why, hello, Thad," Dad said.

"Hi, Mr. Yang," answered Thad.

"You two want a snack?"

"Yes, please."

Eunice was surprised that Thad had said please. He seemed to be much more polite around Dad than he was around her.

Eunice and Thad sat down at the kitchen table. "Don't you see?" Eunice said. "That's our topic. Which is cleaner: a dog's mouth or a human's?"

Thad thought it over. "How are we going to test it out?"

Eunice took out the science experiment packet Ms. Hobart had given them and shook it in front of him. "Don't you read anything?"

"Stop squawking and show me."

Eunice flipped through until she found the page she wanted. She showed it to Thad. "We can get three Petri dishes from the science room and fill them with gelatin. Then we put spit samples from Watson and spit samples from both of us in each of the dishes. Then we see what grows." Eunice sat back, satisfied.

Thad smirked. "I *am* a genius."

Dad returned from the kitchen in time to hear Thad's comment. "You're both geniuses." He gave them each a plate of ice cream sandwiches made from his five-spice snickerdoodles and vanilla ice cream. From the look on Thad's face, Eunice could tell he wasn't going to mind studying at her house after all.

Friday afternoons became their regular science project days. Thad's mom worked late on Fridays and was happy to know where he was. Dad would make them a snack—Thad usually had seconds— then he would leave for work. Thad and Eunice then buckled down for another hour or two.

As their spit morphed into mold and fungus in the Petri dishes, something else changed too. Thad teased her maybe half as much as usual, and Eunice had mostly stopped wishing for him to die. She knew better than to talk about it. She was just glad they weren't fighting so much.

After a few weeks, they started working on the display for their table. Thad cut three large pieces of foam core, then taped the backs with duct tape so the pieces would stand up and fold out. Thad was good at making things.

"Looks good," Eunice said.

"Yeah, not bad," he said, standing back and surveying his work.

Eunice handed him a piece of paper. "What do you think of these changes?"

Thad glanced at it and handed it back. "Looks fine."

"You didn't even read it."

"Did so."

Eunice gave the sheet back to Thad and stood poised with a pencil against the poster board. "Could you read it out loud? I'm going to sketch out the words on the poster while you read."

Thad was silent for a moment. "Why don't you read and I'll sketch?"

"Your printing's terrible," Eunice said, reaching for the paper. "If you can't read it, give it back."

Thad was indignant. "I can read!" He held the paper out of her reach, then brought it back down and stared at it, his brow furrowed. "Our ex-per-i-ment—asks—"

Thad struggled to get the words out. He was following along with his finger. He stopped and looked at her. "It just takes me a little longer, that's all."

"How come no one's ever noticed?"

"I might not be a good reader, but I'm pretty smart." Thad stuck his chin up. "Didn't you notice how you never hear me read out loud in class?"

Thad was right. He always acted up around reading time. Sometimes he'd tease her and they'd get in a fight and end up in the principal's office or outside the classroom for a time-out. Sometimes he'd goof around so much the teacher would send him outside while Eunice finished reading the last passage from the book they were reading. He was *W*; she was *Y*. She always followed him in the reading order. Eunice had never noticed the pattern before.

"Do you think you might have dyslexia?"

"I don't know," Thad said, frowning. "Mom helps me with my homework. One time she talked about getting me tested, and my dad blew up. They got in a big fight." He shrugged. "Grades aren't that important anyway. That's what Dad says."

Eunice shook her head. "He's wrong about that. You should get help. You know Mrs. Bragg at school? She can help you."

Thad folded his arms. "I don't want to talk about it," he said, raising his voice. "It's none of your business." He dropped his gaze and said quietly, "Let's just work on the project, okay?"

Eunice dropped the subject. Thad needed help, but if he didn't want the help, what could she do? "How about if I read it out loud, and you tell me how I should sketch it on the poster?"

"Yeah," said Thad. "That sounds good."

Maybe they didn't agree, but they could still meet in the middle.

After they finished sketching out the poster, Eunice walked Thad to the door. He picked up his backpack and basketball. Eunice eyed the ball. "You probably think this is stupid but—"

"What?" Thad was putting on his sneakers.

"Could you show me how to shoot sometime?"

Thad laughed. "You can't shoot?" Eunice gave him a look. Thad grinned. "Yeah, sure."

18. LEARNING TO SHOOT

Thad stuck to his word, and the next week they headed to the basketball courts after school. Things were going well with their science project, so they decided to skip working on it that afternoon. Eunice thought Thad might back out. They didn't socialize when they were at school, and who knew who might see them on the playground? But Friday turned out to be a good day for shooting hoops. All their classmates were eager to get as far away from school as possible and get ready for the weekend. The courts were deserted.

Thad showed Eunice how to balance the ball in her right hand and steady it with her left. "It's all in the wrist," he said, shooting the ball with a perfect arc into the net. Swoosh.

Thad sank most of his throws. Eunice missed most of hers. Every time she missed, she was sure he'd laugh. But he didn't. He corrected her stance or her throw each time. And when she finally made her first basket, Thad whooped, "Yeah, Eun-i-cycle!" She didn't mind the nickname so much this time.

After about a half hour of practice, they parted ways. When Eunice got home, she could hear her dad stir-frying. The wonderful smell of garlic and green onion wafted through the house.

"Just in time," Dad said. "Could you take this twice-cooked pork to the Warfields'?"

Eunice opened her mouth to whine that she had just seen Thad, but closed it again. Dad had started cooking for the Warfields every few weeks, ever since the black eye incident. She knew her dad still felt bad about her hitting Thad. She did too.

"That boy eats like a horse," Dad said as he scooped the fragrant pork into a plastic tub. "And I know Frances doesn't have time to cook with her hospital job."

Eunice plunked down on a stool. Dad worked just as much as Mrs. Warfield. How did he have time to cook for all of them? He packed up a tub of sticky rice and put lids on both tubs, then placed them into a paper shopping bag printed with *John's Fine Foods*.

Dad handed the bag to Eunice. "By the time you get back, dinner will be ready."

Eunice placed the bag of food in the basket on the front of her bike and rode off. She enjoyed the savory smells wafting out from the bag all the way to Hemlock Street. When she got to Thad's house, she parked her bike on the side of the driveway and grabbed the bag of food. She started toward the front door but heard a basketball bouncing out back. She went around to the backyard to surprise Thad, but stopped in her tracks when she heard two male voices.

"That's not how you do it!" The voice was deeper and older than Thad's.

"Wait. I can do it," Thad said.

Eunice heard the ball bounce, then silence. She pictured it sailing through the air. Bounce. The ball hit the ground. It was out.

"Wait, wait—" Thad said.

The sound of a ball bouncing on the rim. Out again.

"What've you been doing since I've been gone? Boy can't even shoot."

It was Thad's dad! Eunice wondered if he had found a job. She knew she shouldn't eavesdrop, but her feet were glued to the ground. She leaned against the side of the house.

"Give me the ball," Mr. Warfield said.

"Let me try again."

"Don't you talk back, boy. When I say give me the ball, you give me the ball."

Eunice heard what sounded like a smack. She flattened herself against the wall.

The ball started bouncing again. Swoosh.

"See that?" Mr. Warfield said. "That's how you shoot."

Silence.

Eunice had heard enough. She crept toward the front of the house and placed the bag on the front doorstep. Her hand shook as she pushed the doorbell. She didn't wait for a response.

She hopped on her bike and pedaled away as fast as she could. And all the way home, no matter how much she tried, she couldn't get that sound out of her head.

19. THE SCIENCE FAIR

May came in raining cats and dogs. There was so much rain on the day of the science fair that Eunice and Thad worried their display would be ruined. Eunice packed the Petri dishes carefully in a shoe box and wrapped the box in a garbage bag. She carried the package to school like it was the Holy Grail.

The science fair was held after lunch. Hordes of kids packed the schoolyard on account of the students from nearby Ephrata Elementary coming for their annual field trip to the science fair. They ran in and around the crowd of Soap Lake denizens waiting to get inside the gym.

Eunice and Thad were setting up their table when her dad showed up with their display wrapped in trash bags. He had just finished the lunch shift at the Lucky Dragon and had some time before the dinner shift began. Eunice smiled. She wanted her dad to see her win.

"Here you go." Dad took the display out of the bags and set it on the table. He gave Eunice a hug. "I'm proud of you."

Thad stuck out his hand. Dad hugged him instead. "I'm proud of you too."

Thad's face flushed, but Eunice could tell from his smile that Thad was happy to get the hug and the recognition. Would Thad's father come today? She hoped he wouldn't, even though she knew Thad was counting on it.

Dad waved and headed toward the other rows of experiments. "Knock 'em dead, kids!"

Eunice and Thad had just enough time to set up their Petri dishes and display before the doors opened. Swarms of kids and adults streamed into the gym. Over the next hour, they explained their project at least twenty times, maybe more. When the judges came by, Eunice and Thad stood tall, smiled, and shook hands like Ms. Hobart had taught them. As they explained their project, the judges scribbled in their pads. After they left, Eunice breathed a sigh of relief. Thad did too.

"I gotta go," Eunice said. "Can you watch the table?"

"Hurry," Thad said. "I gotta go too."

It was only half a lie. Eunice did have to use the bathroom, but she was also on a mission. She wanted to see what the Hernandez twins had done for their project.

On her way to the twins' table, Eunice passed Jenny and Anna's experiment. A big group of kids stood around their table, chewing and blowing bubbles. Their poster said, "Which brand will give you the biggest bubble?" Eunice scoffed. Bubble gum bubbles? That was so easy even a second grader could do it.

Eunice kept going, and as she wove through the rows of tables, she eventually found the nerds' table. The judges were inspecting their project. Their poster said, "Do you know how much iron is in your cereal? You might be surprised." Eunice's heart dropped a little. Testing iron in cereals? It sounded very scientific.

"As you can see," Jules was saying, "the shredded wheat was the most accurate in showing the correct amount of iron in each serving." The judges were eating it up. Eunice scowled to herself and scurried off.

Finally, she found the twins. They had made a floor out of four different materials—wood, tile, brick, and concrete—and they were bouncing balls. Carson was bouncing a basketball; Callie was bouncing a red jelly ball. Their poster said, "Which ball bounces highest on which surface? And why?"

Eunice grinned while watching the twins explain their experiment. Balls? C'mon. She and Thad had a way better project. Growing fungus and mold was way more scientific. She ran the rest of the way to the bathroom and got back to her table just in time to relieve a nervous-looking Thad.

"Finally," Thad said, exasperated. "What took you so long?"

"Check out the nerds in aisle two and the twins in aisle four. They're our biggest competition."

Thad took off like a shot. Eunice had explained their experiment another ten times by the time he got back. "It's going to be close," Thad said, shaking his head. "Iron in cereal? Those kids are genius."

A xylophone sounded over the loudspeakers. Everyone turned toward the stage at the front of the gym. "Is this thing on?" Mr. Moss smiled and took the mic out of the stand. "Ladies and gentlemen, may I have your attention?"

Eunice, Thad, and the other teams turned to face the stage. Eunice looked around for her dad but couldn't see him in the massive crowd. Sherry Mathers from Bob's Bicycle Shop was standing near the front. Eunice's heart beat faster at the thought of winning the Rainier Cruiser. Her fingers itched, and she could almost feel the handlebars.

"Look." Thad pointed to a tall man in the crowd wearing a Mariners baseball cap. It was Mr. Warfield. He had finally made it. Thad turned away and started fussing with the Petri dishes, smiling to himself.

Eunice's stomach clenched up, seeing how happy it made Thad to have his dad there. She tried to push out of her mind what she had heard at their house.

Eunice's heart pounded harder and harder as Mr. Moss and Mayor Wilkinson approached the podium. Eunice grabbed Thad's arm. Under normal circumstances, she would never have done this. But these circumstances were not normal. Thad must have felt just as nervous because he didn't wrench his arm away or tell her to move it.

Mr. Moss handed the mayor a sheet of paper. Mayor Wilkinson read it and whooped. "Well, I'll be. It's a tie!" Nobody breathed. "First place for the science fair goes to Jules West and Marty Patterson—and to Eunice Yang and Thad Warfield!"

Eunice and Thad jumped up and down, whooping as loud as they could. Thad's smile was so wide, Eunice thought his face would crack in half. Her face probably looked the same.

Mr. Moss held up his hand. "And now for the winners of the One Hundredth Annual Brawn and Brains Contest. Mayor Wilkinson, will you do the honors?" He handed Mayor Wilkinson another sheet of paper.

Eunice closed her eyes. If anyone had looked at her, they would have thought she was praying, but she was only trying not to faint.

Mayor Wilkinson read the sheet and whooped again. "Folks, you're not going to believe this. It's another tie! Callie and Carson Hernandez and"—he paused—"Eunice Yang and Thad Warfield!"

Everyone was screaming but Eunice couldn't hear a thing. She made a mental note to get her ears checked. Again, everything seemed like it was in slow motion. When her hearing finally kicked in, she saw that Thad was jumping up and down and screaming, and soon, she was too.

Eunice's heart swelled at the thought of having the Rainier Cruiser for her very own. She pumped her fist in the air. Hooyeah! The Cruiser was hers!

Mr. Moss held up his hand. After a long time, the crowd calmed down.

"As you know, only one team can win The Contest. We have planned for the rare possibility that there might be a tie." He motioned to Eunice, Thad, Carson, and Callie. "If the two winning teams could please step forward for the sudden death elimination challenge."

20. EUNICE'S CHOICE

"Ladies first. Eunice and Callie, please come up on stage."

Why ladies first? This wasn't a lifeboat. Why couldn't the boys go first for a change? Eunice approached the stage, feeling a little woozy. *Breathe. Put one foot in front of the other.* Callie beamed and waved at the crowd like she was Miss America. Eunice wanted to wipe the smile right off her face.

"I'm going to flip a coin. The team that wins the toss gets to choose the challenge." Mr. Moss flipped a quarter in the air. "Call it."

"Heads!" Callie yelled before Eunice could say anything.

The quarter spun in slow motion. It took forever to land in Mr. Moss's open palm. He flipped the hand with the quarter onto the back of his other hand and showed it to them. "Tails!"

Callie's face fell. Eunice grinned.

She heard her dad and Mr. Oliver whooping in the crowd. Mr. Moss faced her. "This is for the win, Eunice. You have two choices. Will it be a spelling bee or free throws?"

Eunice's heart jumped into her throat. She would

have preferred battling sharks in a tank. Her head spun.

"Please, can we have some quiet?" Mr. Moss said into the mic.

The crowd calmed down a bit. Eunice could finally hear herself think. Then it became so quiet that she could hear her heart pounding and the blood rushing through her veins. She started to feel woozy again.

Callie shifted her weight from side to side. She and Carson were practically cracking their faces in two from smiling. Either way she chose, the twins would do fine. They could both spell, and they could both play basketball. Eunice's heart sank.

She looked at Thad. His face was frozen and his brow was shiny with sweat. She knew then what to do. Looking right at Thad, she leaned into the mic. "We'll take free throws."

Relief washed over Thad's face. He smiled at Eunice. She smiled back.

The crowd started chanting, "Free throws! Free throws! Free throws!" The science projects were cleared from one side of the gym to reveal a half basketball court.

"Thank you, ladies," Mr. Moss said. "You may join your teammates on the court. You will each get two chances to make a free throw. Each basket is worth one point. The team with the most points wins."

This time it was boys first. Another quarter was tossed. Carson won. He stepped up and bounced the ball. The first shot went in. Second shot—IN. Carson punched the air with his fist.

Thad stepped up. He focused on the basket. Bounce, bounce, bounce. Swoosh. Bounce, bounce, bounce. Swoosh. Thad whooped and high-fived Eunice.

Callie was next. She bounced the ball for what seemed like hours. Eunice wanted to smack it out of her hand. First shot. IN. Another long set of bounces. Finally, she shot again, hit the rim, and it went—IN. The crowd roared.

Someone passed the ball to Eunice. She stepped into place, trying to remember what Thad had taught her. *It's all in the wrist.* Eunice bounced the ball, balanced it in her right hand, and shot. She held her breath. It went—IN. She exhaled.

Eunice bounced the ball. Balanced it just right. *It's all in the wrist. It's all in the wrist.* She held her breath and shot. The ball hit the rim. And it was—

OUT.

Callie's scream drowned out everything else.

Eunice's heart dropped clear past her stomach and into her high-tops.

"The winners of the One Hundredth Annual Brawn and Brains Contest are Carson and Callie Hernandez!" Mr. Moss's voice boomed out from the podium. "Second place goes to Eunice Yang and Thad Warfield! And third place goes to Jules West and Marty Patterson!"

The three teams walked up to the podium to collect their ribbons. The Hernandez twins got blue ribbons. Eunice and Thad got red. Jules and Marty got white.

Eunice held her ribbon limply in her hand and blinked to keep the tears from falling. She watched Sherry Mathers hand gift certificates to Carson and Callie. It was too much. She turned away.

"That's a mighty fine ribbon you got there."

Eunice looked up to see her dad. He hugged her, lifting her off the ground. She finally let her tears fall. "I'm so proud of you," he whispered.

"Right good show, Eunice!" Mr. Oliver said, giving her a hug. "I can't wait to tell Watson. He's going to be elated that you won first place in the fair with *his* saliva."

Eunice wiped her eyes with her sleeve. Good old Mr. Oliver. Good old Watson.

An apparition in black stepped forward. Eunice almost fell over. It was the Black Widow! In daylight! Outside of her yard! Eunice glanced around to see if any other kids noticed.

"Surprised to see me, eh?" Mrs. Lebowitz said.

"Well, yeah."

Mrs. Lebowitz laughed, a very bubbly and contagious laugh. Eunice couldn't help but laugh too. Her dad and Mr. Oliver joined in. For a second, Eunice stepped back, held her breath, and took a photo of the scene with her mind. Click. Recorded forever.

"Pie à la mode at the Yang residence," Dad said. They all cheered. He turned to Eunice. "You can invite Thad too, if you like."

In all the hullabaloo, Eunice had completely forgotten about Thad. As they joined the crowd streaming out of the gym, Eunice spied him walking with his mom and dad. Mrs. Warfield had her arm around him.

Eunice wondered if Thad was upset about not winning. She tried to catch his eye just as Mr. Warfield looked over and locked eyes with her. His glare said it all.

He didn't scare her though. On a different day, he probably would have. But today, Dad and Mr. Oliver and even Mrs. Lebowitz had her back. Even more than that, she was a contender. Even if they hadn't won, they had been a team. A real team. No one could take that away.

Eunice lifted her chin and looked Mr. Warfield in the eye. Mr. Warfield turned back around. A moment later, Thad looked over his shoulder. His eyes lit up when he saw Eunice, and he waved. She waved back.

"It's okay," Eunice said. "I'll save him a slice."

Then they all stepped out into the sunlight.

21. THE PACKAGE

Sitting up in the old oak tree with the sun blazing down, Eunice watched Mrs. Lebowitz peering through her bushes with a magnifying glass. She wore an old floppy straw hat. It reminded Eunice of Ms. Hobart's grandfather's hat. Instead of squinting and scowling at Eunice like she used to, now Mrs. Lebowitz squinted, smiled, and waved. Eunice waved back.

Summer vacation was here, but for once in her life, Eunice wasn't happy about it. The end of the school year had left her with more questions than answers.

Thad had moved away.

On the last day of school, Eunice kept looking at Thad's empty desk, wondering when he was going to show up. After the pledge of allegiance, Ms. Hobart had announced that Mrs. Warfield called early in the morning to explain that they were moving to Montana, where Mr. Warfield had found a job. No wonder Buzz looked so hangdog.

It was hard for Eunice to digest. She felt like crying and laughing at the same time. She had finally gotten what she wanted. Thad Warfield was gone. She

126

had spent so much time wishing for it, she didn't realize when she had stopped.

Eunice heard kids running down the street. She heard girls laughing, and it made her think of Jenny, who was back in summer camp with Anna. The school year was bearable without a best friend, but summer sure was lonely without one. She wondered if Buzz felt the same way.

A dog barked. "What ho, Watson! Wait for me, old boy." Eunice smiled to herself. Watson was taking Mr. Oliver out for his walk.

She swung down from the oak branch and did fifteen pull-ups before she dropped to the ground. Eunice didn't have to train for The Contest anymore but she still liked doing them. She liked being one of the only girls who could beat the boys.

If only doing more pull-ups could help her get the Rainier Cruiser. But all hope was not lost. Mr. Oliver and Mrs. Lebowitz were going to pay her every week to help them clean up their yards. Dad even said he would match whatever she was able to save. It would take months to scrimp and pinch, but Eunice figured she could have the Cruiser by next year.

Eunice went into the house and headed for the kitchen. She made herself a lime rickey, put a straw in the glass, and then went out front to sit on the stoop. Just as she slurped the last sugary lime bits from the bottom of the glass, the mailman stepped up.

Eunice stopped slurping and looked up. "Hi, Keith."

"Hey there, Eunice. You got something today." He handed her a little brown package, along with some letters, and continued on his route.

Eunice leafed through the stack. The mail was for her dad. All bills. She put them aside.

The package was addressed to her. The printing was terrible. There was no return address. Eunice held her breath as she ripped it open. Nestled in foam peanuts lay a shiny silver bike bell emblazoned with a bright red cherry. She breathed out in awe.

Did Dad send it? Or Mr. Oliver? Or Mrs. Lebowitz?

She lifted it out. It was beautiful. It was exactly like the one on the Rainier Cruiser. She flicked the bell and heard the delightful high-pitched ring. Who could have sent it? Eunice looked back at the box. The postmark said MT. MT stood for Montana. Eunice furrowed her brow. She didn't know anyone in Montana.

Then it dawned on her.

She saw him in her mind. A boy short for his age, wiry and fast like a coyote. At first glance, you thought you could whip him. But you'd be wrong.

This time, Eunice didn't scowl or wish this boy dead. This time, thinking of Thad Warfield made her smile.

ACKNOWLEDGMENTS

First, I want to thank the people who helped make this book a reality. I raise my fist in tribute to my awesome beta readers, Brenda Olson and Mary Bell (members of the KAC: Kick-Ass Critiquers), Robin Gaphni, and Marcus Donner; my superb editor, Julie Klein; and my talented cover designer, Kit Foster. I doff my hat to editor Connie Hsu for reading the first iteration of Eunice in my picture book, *The Terrible Pirate Chang*, at the 2009 SCBWI Western Washington Conference and encouraging me to turn it into a novel.

Second, I raise my frosty glass of lime rickey to my terrific teachers Donna Bergman, Meg Lippert, and Brenda Z. Guiberson from the 2007-2008 University of Washington Extension Writing for Children program; and to Brian McDonald, my friend, mentor, and teacher who has taught me more about storytelling than anyone else.

Third, many magical muddy thanks to Evie Wilkinson, retired secretary of Soap Lake Elementary School, who gave me an excellent tour of the school; the librarian and the volunteer at the Soap Lake Public Library, who both told me interesting tidbits about the town; and the spirited volunteer who toured me around the Masquers Theater, all back in March 2010.

Finally, I send out a huge plate of five-spice snickerdoodle ice cream sandwiches to all my friends and family for their support and encouragement. Thanks especially to my parents, Tilden and Mary Cheng; my brother, Steve Cheng; my in-laws, Charlene "Char" Donner and Mark "Mr. Mark" Donner; my friends Erik "Boesche" Schweighofer and Ed "Edgy" Cosgrove for always believing in me, and Linda Ando for introducing me as a writer even before I thought of myself as one; and last but not least, my amazing husband and first reader, Marcus Donner.

ABOUT THE AUTHOR

Peg Cheng was born in Pasadena, California, grew up south of there in Huntington Beach, and now lives in Seattle, Washington, with her husband and a very special Scotch plaid frog. She has worked as a fabric cutter, a bus parts counter, a tennis clothing seller, a laboratory assistant, a public toilet researcher, a communications director, a career counselor, an academic adviser, and in twenty-seven other jobs.

When she's not writing stories, Peg helps people navigate the treacherous, shark-infested waters of applying to law school, reads a ton, walks a lot, grows vegetables, travels when she can, practices qigong and yoga, and indulges in crazy socks.

Peg loves hearing from her readers! Follow her on Twitter @pegcheng and connect with her at pegcheng.com.

WORDS HAVE POWER

Word-of-mouth is crucial for every author. If you enjoyed this book, it would be greatly appreciated if you could write a review on the site where you found it, even if it's just a line or two. Reviews make all the difference in the world. Thank you for your support.

44217468R00087

Made in the USA
Charleston, SC
17 July 2015